*No way out . . .*

Slowly she looked back up the stairs and unconsciously moved back against the wall while she caught her breath. She counted four railings. Above her, at the fourth railing, a shadow moved against the wall. It stopped. How much sound did her breathing make? She pressed her hand to her mouth and then to her heart.

She turned around. The small pane of glass in the middle of the basement door was blocked from the outside by what looked like cardboard. She pushed the bar to open it. It gave less than an inch. Someone had deliberately shut her in.

# HEAR NO EVIL

Death in the Afternoon
Missing!
A Time of Fear
Dead and Buried

# HEAR NO EVIL

## A Time of Fear

*Kate Chester*

**SCHOLASTIC INC.**
New York Toronto London Auckland Sydney

ISBN 0-590-67328-9

Copyright © 1996 by Leslie Davis Guccione.
All rights reserved. Published by Scholastic Inc.

12 11 10 9 8 7 6 5 4 3 2 1        6 7 8 9/9 0 1/0

Printed in the U.S.A.                    01

First Scholastic printing, October 1996

To the Reader:

Sara Howell is profoundly, postlingually deaf (meaning she lost her hearing after she learned to speak). She is fluent in American Sign Language (ASL), and English. She can read lips.

When a character speaks, quotation marks are used: "Watch out for that bus!" When a character signs, *italics* are used to indicate ASL: *Watch out for that bus!* Quotation marks and *italics* indicate the character is signing and speaking simultaneously: *"Watch out for that bus!"*

Unless the sign is described (for example: Sara circled her heart. *I'm sorry . . .* ), the italicized words are translations of ASL into English, not literal descriptions of the grammatical structure of American Sign Language.

## Chapter 1

Sara Howell pulled her crew team windbreaker over her shirt and Lycra racing shorts. She scanned the river as she jostled her way through the spectators milling along the banks. Pain and exhaustion slowed her pace and finally forced her to stop. For the second time she looked over her shoulder as she did a quick set of exercises to soothe her calf muscles.

Her heart still pounded. It's the exercise, she told herself, as she glanced left, then right. She pressed a fist against her ribs. Too much exercise after the rigors of the rowing competition must be what kept her pulse racing and her adrenaline pumping. However, exercise couldn't account for the eerie feeling of foreboding.

Maybe it was concern for Steve. Her detective brother, who was also her guardian, was involved in a high-profile police case. He kept details from her, but he'd let it slip that his tire had been punctured, brazenly, right in the parking area in front of the precinct station. She'd worried about him even before she'd left for the weekend. However, Steve was in Radley and she was here, hundreds of miles up the Buckeye River. His undercover police work didn't account for her creeping-up-the-back-of-the-neck chills, or the sensation that she was being watched.

The High Pines Regatta was the largest rowing competition in the region. Its annual November date marked the end of the season and hundreds of competitors, school officials, and parents were scattered over the two-and-a-half-mile course, from the launching site upstream at the local club's boathouse, to the finish line where Sara stood. She scoffed. Everyone was focused on the water and the last events of the day. No one was looking at her. In fact, she was lucky to be here at all.

The Radley Academy crew team had been scheduled to leave for the regatta directly from school on Friday. Coach Barns had pulled Sara out of study hall to tell her that a last-minute double check had turned up neither the permission slip nor medical forms necessary for her to compete. Despite Sara's protests that they'd been handed in on time, the only solution was fresh forms, signed — again — by her brother. Steve had saved the day, but had to be roused from sleep after his late-night shift.

The bad luck didn't account for the chills, either. Nothing more had happened. The regatta had been a huge success for Radley Academy. Sara had helped the eight-women shell, or Women's Eight as it was called, bring in a silver medal. She focused on the victory to dismiss her uneasiness.

The spectators were watching the final events on the river or caught up in conversation. Mouths moved; arms gestured. Mouths, arms, hands, eyebrows: Sometimes the hearing world seemed like nothing but disjointed body parts. No one was looking at her. No one included her. Even her teammates back at the landing docks were caught up in a world she was still trying to fit into. *Relax,* she added in American Sign Language to herself.

Sara adjusted the band that held her shoulder-length hair into a French braid and started down the slope to the water. She strained to catch a glimpse of the rowers and shake off whatever this eerie feeling was. She straightened her shoulders. Hearing wasn't necessary to feel safe, and she didn't need sound to appreciate the beauty of the rowing shells as the competitors skimmed toward the finish line. Gingerly she left the grass and made her way onto the stone wall that lined the river.

Rowers, teammates . . . there was plenty to divert her attention. Next to her a knot of high school rowers punched the air and jumped as they cheered for their team. Sara smiled, but as she watched, a firm tap on her shoulder threw her heart against her ribs again. She spun around, lost her balance, and shoved her arms out to fend off the rocks. As her foot slipped on the uneven stones, the tap turned to a grab. Michael Lenza yanked her up onto the grass and into his arms. Whatever he had said was lost as he turned his head.

The tall, athletic rower reluctantly let go. "I've been chasing you all the way from the parking lot," he said.

"You've been watching me?" she asked as clearly as possible.

He frowned in confusion.

Never mind. Sara tapped her ear. "Deaf. Couldn't hear you." Since she'd met him Friday night, his expressions wavered from curious to irritated. It made her wonder why he insisted on being so attentive. At sixteen Sara rowed for Radley Academy, one of her city's private schools. Mike said he was a senior and rowed for his high school in the Radley suburb of Hillsboro. Beyond that she hadn't discovered much that they had in common. At the moment it didn't matter. She was glad for his company.

"We took second place," she said, grateful that the chills had finally dissipated.

Mike frowned as he knotted his jacket around his waist.

Sara held up two fingers. "Second in the Women's Eight."

He finally understood, and smiled. "I got it. Second. Congratulations. I saw the press interviewing you."

Sara looked back at the television van parked at the edge of the judges' stand. The Radley media had insisted on an interview, one for their live remote television broadcast back to the city, and another for the Sunday paper. "Human interest," they'd called it, for the hometown fans. Frankly, she'd had enough of their human interest stories. The high-profile death of her detective father had thrown her into the spotlight too many times already.

This afternoon she'd cooperated because the other rowers from her team, including her best friend Keesha Fletcher, had insisted. It gave her a chance to show that deafness didn't inhibit her. She also hoped media exposure might help to educate hearing kids . . . like Mike Lenza.

She'd met the sandy-haired athlete as the teams arrived at the High Pines boathouse for registration and a pasta dinner. When he'd learned she was deaf he'd seemed curious, intrigued, then determined to hold her interest. At least that was her interpretation. She'd only been back in Radley — and in the hearing world — since her father's death at the end of August.

Except for vacations, the Edgewood School for the Deaf, a community as much as a school, had been her home since her mother's death six years earlier. Now that she'd lost her father as well, she wanted — and needed — to be closer to 22-year-old Steve, her only sibling.

Understanding Mike took diligence and concentration on his body language. She knew he had to put as much effort, if not more, into understanding her. As he helped her regain her balance, she signed, *thank you*. She hoped he didn't interpret her concentration as romantic interest. She'd thought about mentioning that she dated Bret Sanderson, but figured time would solve everything. Season competition was over. The teams would disperse after these final events.

This evening, as soon as the Radley Academy rowing shells were secured to the trailer and the team had some dinner, the school vans would head for home. It was a four-hour drive and Sara intended to sleep the whole way. Chances of running into Mike Lenza after today were slim.

## Chapter 2

A loose piece of her dark hair worked its way out of her braid and she tucked it behind her ear. "I'm exhausted." She pointed toward the river. "I want to watch the masters' division. My coach is rowing." She started to lead Mike back to the rocky river bank. He held her back.

"Lunch. You said we'd have lunch together."

"Important event." *Important.* She made circles with her thumbs and index fingers, then brought her hands together.

He shrugged that he didn't understand.

Sara pointed to the closest food booth. "Let's buy something over there. Eat and watch." This time he understood.

As Mike ordered for both of them, she studied him for more signs of annoyance or disappointment. Surely he hadn't thought lunch meant a secluded picnic somewhere. She was beginning to wonder just what he did think.

"I can drive you home," he said as they returned to their spot at the water's edge. He pantomimed holding a steering wheel.

Sara shook her head. "School van from here to our motel."

"No. Back to Radley. I'll drive you back. Hillsboro's just across the river."

Sara shook her head. "Thank you, but I have to go with my team. Strict school rules."

"Break the rules." His green gaze was penetrating.

She looked at him curiously. He really thought she'd risk team suspension for a four-hour ride home with a boy she hardly knew? She circled her heart, the sign for *sorry.* "I'll go home with my team. You'll go home with yours."

"Do you always play by the rules?"

She tapped his jaw with her fingertips to get him to look directly at her when he spoke.

He flushed and smiled, but it added to her frustration. She wasn't flirting! To read his lips she had to turn away from the river and the competition. This wasn't the time for a drawn out conversation, especially one that bordered on an argument. She tried to be playful as she pointed at the racers. She tried to convey: Watch with me.

"Come on," he repeated. "Why jam into the stuffy van when you can ride back with me?"

Deafness had its advantages. She put on her best vague, I-didn't-catch-that face, then turned to watch the rowers as they sliced through the water on their way to the finish line.

Empty apartment. It was the first thing Sara thought of as the lurch of the school van woke her up. Coach Barns was pumping the brakes as she maneuvered onto the shoulder of the country road. Sara didn't need hearing to guess they had a flat tire. Late dinner had delayed their departure. And now this. Her brother would leave for the police station at 9:45 P.M. She'd be lucky if she got home by midnight. Maybe she should have returned with Mike.

Sara sighed and closed her eyes again. The Howells' odd schedules and an often-empty apartment were two of the reasons her father had found her a secure boarding school. Now the apartment and her brother's erratic hours were part of her adjustment to life in Radley, the part she hated.

The van tilted slightly as the coach found a safe stretch of road and parked. Sara was sitting next to Liz Martinson who had learned some ASL, but without streetlights it was too dark to read hands or lips well. For fluency she needed Keesha. Her fellow rower and best friend had started ASL lessons with her ten years ago when meningitis had left Sara profoundly deaf. Keesha was African-American and lived with her family in the apartment across the hall from Sara and Steve. But Keesha was in the other van.

Sara could have also used Bret Sanderson. Not only was he fluent in ASL, because his parents were deaf, his shoulder would have been wonderful to snuggle against. Unfortunately Bret didn't go to Radley Academy and he didn't row. He was a star basketball player for Radley's rival, Penham School.

The van's overhead light snapped on and the coach opened the door and made an announcement. "Flat tire?" Sara asked Liz.

The redhead nodded and signed, *Everybody out.* "Coach Barns said she's calling the auto club from her cellular phone. They'll send somebody to change the tire. In the meantime . . ." Liz shrugged and nodded in the direction of the grassy field, chilly under the rising moon.

Sara joined the others on a dark stretch of meadow. Except for the dot of window lights in a distant house, and the occasional stream of headlights when a car passed, the night was shadowed, gray. Peaceful, Sara tried to believe, in order to chase the chills.

In broad daylight with hundreds of people, she'd been filled with weird feelings. Now, stranded on a country road with nothing but a handful of classmates, stars and shadowed rockbound fields, it was impossible to relax. It won't quit. Whatever had plagued her since

Friday night held fast in the inky silence. The night could have been comforting, almost romantic in its shade and silhouettes. It was too dark to read anyone's lips. Instead she hugged her knees and watched the stars, trying to calm her nerves.

By midnight the moon was overhead. It cast bright, brittle light on the blacktop as Coach Barns finally pulled into the deserted Shelter Island boathouse parking lot. The first Radley Academy van, as well as the other area teams that had competed, were long gone. The only sign of life was dozing parents in their cars waiting for the late arrivals.

With one last round of hugs, congratulations, and thanks to the coach, the rowers grabbed their duffel bags and backpacks and headed for the cars. Coach Barns chatted briefly with the parents, saw that everyone was accounted for, then eased the van out of the lot.

Liz and Sara had parked side by side. "I'll sleep all day tomorrow," Liz said under the dome light of her car.

Sara smiled and nodded. *Me, too,* she signed. *See you. School. Monday.* She waved. If they'd been on time, Sara would have driven Keesha home, but by now her friend had probably been in bed for hours. Now that she was alone, Sara stayed just long enough to admire the splintered moonlight on the lapping water of the Buckeye River. There hadn't been much peace since her turbulent return to Radley and she stood still, inhaling the autumn air and enjoying the comfortable silence. The chill helped to wake her up. She needed to be alert for the ten-minute drive from the island to her apartment building.

Sara smiled and raised her face to the moonlight. Second place in the high school division of the Women's Eight. Wait till Steve found out. Wait till she told Bret. She threw her arms out on either side of her, yawned, and stretched her well-worked muscles. Despite her aches, she felt good, wonderful in fact.

Sara spun on her sneakers with her arms still wide. As she pivoted toward the river in the cold, silent air, she smacked directly into someone a head taller and twice as broad. He'd been standing directly behind her. Her scream was a muffled cry that stuck in her throat.

# Chapter 3

Sara stared at the baseball cap pulled low over the face. She was gripped at the shoulders, as if he were trying to stand her up. He let go of one arm and yanked his cap off. "Sara!"

She blinked and choked back the tears of fright. It was Mike Lenza, staring at her as if she'd lost her mind.

She glared at the familiar face, barely relieved. He knew good and well she couldn't hear anyone behind her. For the second time since noon, he'd terrified her. She tried to read in his features that this had been a joke. It was too dark.

"Sara," he repeated.

She caught her breath and spoke with angry gestures to her ears. ASL was useless. "I can't hear you behind me. You scared me to death. It's after midnight. Why are you still here?"

He looked perplexed. "Here? I'm here to wait for you."

"Me? Why?" She sucked in a huge breath to calm her heart. "It's very late. Time to go home." She tapped her watch to make sure he understood.

Once again he put his hand on her arm. "Leave your car here. I'll drive you home, make sure you're safe. You can pick it up tomorrow."

Sara's heart continued to thump painfully. "No, I'm fine. Don't worry about me. I don't need to leave my car. Your own family must be waiting." She glanced around the empty parking lot, searching for someone — anyone — who could help her get rid of Mike. But there was no one. She hoped she didn't look as anxious as she felt. When she touched Mike's arm to keep his attention, he put his hand over hers.

"Mike, I have a friend —" She paused at

his blank expression. Sara took another breath. It was hard enough making him understand her in daylight. This was impossible. She pulled him into the light from the security lamps on the corner of the boathouse, but as she looked up at him again, he leaned over. He misunderstood! It was too late. Mike kissed her.

Her cheeks burned and she shook her head. "I'm dating someone."

Mike studied her. "What? Who?"

"Bret Sanderson." She said it as clearly as she could.

"Is it serious?"

Sara paused. It was too soon to feel serious. For now dating Bret Sanderson felt comfortable and secure, neither of which she was feeling in the deserted, shadowed parking lot. She tapped her watch again. "I have to go. You, too. Thanks for waiting for me."

If she'd bordered on being rude, maybe that's what it would take. She managed to smile, but then turned firmly to her car. Mike tapped her once more on the shoulder.

"I'll follow. Make sure you get home safely."

She thrust one thumb to the left and one to the right to indicate that they lived in opposite directions. "No. I'll be fine." She gave him a small wave and got into her car.

Her chills were back. She grimaced. All afternoon she'd felt as if she were being scrutinized by a hundred pairs of eyes. Worse, not once but twice Mike Lenza had scared the breath out of her and she'd never suspected a thing. With a last wave for him, still next to her car, Sara started the ignition and drove toward the bridge that spanned the Buckeye River. Her left turn onto it would take her off the island into Radley. Mike Lenza's right turn would lead him to Hillsboro. She didn't wait to see which way he turned. She didn't even wait to find out where he'd parked his car.

By the time Sara reached the Radley city streets, she was used to the steady glow of a distant set of headlights in her rearview mirror. Mike was seeing her home whether she wanted him to or not. She should have guessed he would ignore her advice. She knew she should temper her irritation with gratitude, but she was as exhausted by his attention as she was by the strenuous weekend of the rowing regatta.

I'll be home soon, she told herself as she reached the last stoplight, then crossed the avenue to the handsome apartment building. Half a block behind, Mike's car stopped. She passed the front entrance of Thurston Court and turned into the alley. As she pushed the tenants' garage button and waited for the metal door to rise, the bright blue compact car that had seen her safely home slid into view under a streetlight.

Good manners told her she should roll down her window and thank him. Common sense said it would only add encouragement. He'd followed her home to keep her from being uneasy. How could she explain that he was the reason she sat gripping her steering wheel, willing the heavy steel parking entrance to open? Sara swallowed her irritation and drove into the building without looking back at the street.

She parked in the Howells' reserved space; as expected, Steve's spot was empty. Her heart fell. She was alone. Keesha's company would have taken the edge off the emptiness.

She wasn't scared . . . fright was something she was determined not to give in to. She sorted her keys and dragged her duffel bag through the heavy steel fire doors and past the storage rooms to the elevators. The harsh overhead light was on in the laundry room, but there was no sign of life.

As a child, she'd liked the thrill of the creepy basement atmosphere, but she'd usually had her mother's hand in hers, or her father's reassuring voice at her side. All that had changed. No mother, no father, no one's voice ever again. The only thing that hadn't changed was the basement. She shook off the mood as she reached the elevator. Home soon. Seven flights up.

She pushed the button and waited for the elevator as it slid down the cables and arrived behind the polished doors. Mike Lenza is inside the elevator waiting for you, Sara thought to herself.

The unwanted image had popped into her head with such force, Sara cringed and leaned back against the wall. She ached for a hug from Bret; even her brother's fractured attempts at ASL would have been welcome.

The elevator doors slid back. Her adrenaline rush was as strong as if she were back at the finish line at High Pines. Empty. Of course it's empty. Just because you're expecting figments of your imagination to materialize doesn't mean they will. She poked the button for the seventh floor and pulled her duffel bag in with her.

*Did you miss me?* Sara knelt and woke up Tuck, her golden retriever trained as a hearing ear dog. She needed company. The hall lamp by the door was on, as usual, and Steve had added two in the living room. She was grateful. The long halls and empty rooms still made her uncomfortable when she was by herself.

Tuck got up and shook himself, then followed Sara down to her bedroom. She dropped her duffel bag and purse on her guest bed. Tuck sniffed and stretched, then curled back into sleep at the foot of her bed, his usual place.

Sara crossed the hall to the den and snapped on the light to check her telecommunications machine for messages. The message light was dark on the TTY, and on the regular answering machine. She wrote a quick note to prop on the front hall table for Steve.

> I'm home safe and sound. A flat tire
> delayed us. We took second place!
> Tell you about it tomorrow. I'm ex-
> hausted.
>
> XXXX Sara

As she left, she glanced out the window. The seventh-floor view was of sky and roofs and the street that ran in front of the entrance. Traffic was scarce, but there it was: the blue compact car, idling at the stoplight. She could see the hood clearly. As she watched, Michael Lenza pulled around the corner. There was no mistaking the model or the shade of blue as it passed under the street-lights. Her chills returned. Her scalp tingled.

He was good-looking, perfectly nice. He was overattentive, for sure, but she should be flattered that he cared. She glanced at her watch. None of her mental arguments calmed her; it had been a full ten minutes since she'd pulled into the garage. He'd circled the block, or idled out front. Worse, maybe he'd parked down there and stared up at the windows to see what light snapped on. She yanked the shades closed. *Go home,* she signed to the window. *Stay home.*

She glanced back at the TTY and wished it weren't too late to call Bret. Since both his parents were deaf, they were as sensitive to the blinking light of their TTY as hearing people were to the ring of the phone. She shook her head. It was nearly one A.M. Calling would wake up the whole household. She'd have to wait until morning. Suddenly the overhead light blinked, throwing Sara's pulse back into overdrive. She turned to find her brother in the doorway.

His expression became immediately apologetic and he circled his heart. *Sorry. I didn't mean to frighten you. I worked an early shift. We cracked the case.* He fumbled over his limited ASL vocabulary. "Computer fraud. A group working out of Cleveland."

*You're okay? No more threats?* Sara signed back.

*Don't worry. I'm fine.*

*No more slashed tires?*

*Nothing! Relax.* He tried to continue in sign, then gave up and nodded toward the window. Concern darkened his blue eyes. "Just now you signed: Go home. Who's out there?"

*No one.*

*Someone,* Steve signed.

She sighed. "Just a boy I met at the regatta. Mike Lenza." Steve frowned in confusion. "Mike. *L-E-N-Z-A,*" She finger spelled his name and spoke as clearly as she could while she signed. "Hillsboro," she said because she had no sign for the name of the town. *"Followed me home to make sure all was safe. I was just shooing him away."* She made the motion with her hands.

*Nice guy?*

*I guess so. Not Bret,* she used his name sign: *B* plus *VOICE,* given to him by his parents because he could hear and speak.

Steve smiled.

She stayed in the den long enough to tell Steve about their win. He gave her a congratulatory hug and went to the kitchen for a snack. The exhaustion she'd been fighting since lunch crashed in on her, but she parted the curtains and looked down at the street one last time. There was no sign of the blue car. She crossed the hall to Tuck, and to the comfort of her own bed.

Chapter 4

# Chapter 4

*D*EAF ROWER TRIUMPHS! Bret Sanderson signed the headline of the Radley *Gazette*'s sports section, then pulled Sara into a hug. She stayed wrapped in his arms, feeling the steady thumping of his heart, then she playfully pushed him away and ushered him into the apartment.

*Nice article,* he added as he handed her an extra copy.

The piece resulted from her interview at the regatta and focused on her ability as an athlete and the second-place medal Radley's women rowers had won. It also mentioned the adversity in her life, the death of her father as well as her deafness. Under the headline and above the copy was a picture of her smiling in victory with Liz, Keesha, and the rest of the team behind her.

*Maybe it'll encourage some deaf kids. That's why I gave the interview,* she signed back.

It was four o'clock Sunday afternoon. Her homework was finished and she was looking forward to a few hours of just hanging out with Bret. Because of his persistence she'd half expected a phone call from Mike even though she'd done nothing to explain how he could use the relay operator to speak with her through her TTY. The less encouragement the Hillsboro rower had, the better. For all she knew, he didn't think she could use a phone. Hours earlier she'd decided not to mention him to Bret. Mike meant nothing to her and it would seem like she was trying to make Bret jealous. Now she stood on tiptoes and kissed Bret, who was relaxed and handsome in jeans and a flannel shirt.

*Thanks! Was that for anything special?* he signed.

*Just for being you. It's nice to be back in Radley.*

*Life was pretty dull without you.*

*Dull? Aren't you the one who always lectures me on too much excitement?*

*Too much danger,* Bret replied as some of the playfulness left his brown eyes. *There have been some pretty terrifying moments since I met you —*

Sara kissed him again to keep him from going into details over past events. *No lectures. I have a brother for that.*

Bret held her close for a long moment then nodded. *I'm just glad you're back.*

They spent the afternoon in the den with Steve watching a college football game on television. When it was over they crossed the hall to the Fletchers' to see if Keesha wanted to go out for pizza. Sara watched as Bret talked to Keesha about the regatta. Not once all afternoon had Sara had to ask Bret if she'd misunderstood him. Not once had he signed anything she didn't want to know. She was already relaxed. The eerie feeling had vanished.

*DEAF ROWER TRIUMPHS.* Keesha Fletcher signed the headline excitedly. *I can't believe we got second place.*

*I can. I nearly collapsed from the effort,* Sara replied.

*Tall, athletic . . . you're a natural,* Keesha added before turning down the pizza invitation because of a Monday morning math test.

*. . . then in overtime, I made the basket. What a game.* Bret pressed his raised palms away from his face to sign, *Fantastic! Come watch my game on Friday. We could do something afterward. Saturday my family's flying to Michigan for my grandparents' fiftieth wedding anniversary. I won't be back till Wednesday.*

*Sure. I'd love to watch.* Sara smiled at the animation in his face and the warmth in his brown eyes. They'd just been out for pizza and after struggling to communicate with Mike Lenza, Sara was more grateful than ever for Bret and his fluency in ASL. Since she'd left Edgewood, Bret and Keesha had become her link to the hearing world.

Too soon he pulled his family car up to the Thurston Court entrance. Sara turned in her seat. *Harvest Dance at school —*

Bret nodded. *Keesha told me about it. I thought you'd never ask. I'd love to go.*

Sara laughed and shook her head. *I'm not planning to go. I just wanted you to know about it in case somebody else asks you.*

Bret tapped his ear.

Sara nodded, *yes,* she was self-conscious about her deafness. *School gym. Everybody there,* she signed. *Not for me.*

Bret's smile was warm. *Sure it's for you. We danced at Liz Martinson's riverboat party.*

*Just a few times. Not so many kids there, either.*

He raised his index finger. *I'll make a deal. You invite me and we'll dance a few times — behind the bleachers, out in the hall by the lockers. No one will see us and we don't need music.*

*Very funny.*

*I'll just tap out a beat on your head.* He rapped his index finger on her forehead in a steady rhythm. *The rest of the time we'll talk to the chaperons.*

*Very funny,* she signed again. Bret was funny . . . and kind and understanding.

Sometimes it felt as though he got right inside her head as he second-guessed her self-doubts.

He touched her cheek. *It'll be fun. You'll see.*

*It's true. With you, everything's fun,* she replied. *And I even have a dress already, from a party at Edgewood.*

*There, see? I knew you'd been thinking about it.*

*I had not! The dress isn't even clean.*

Bret pointed over his shoulder. *No excuse. There's a cleaners right on the corner. Run upstairs and get it. We'll drop it off.*

Sara laughed. *They're closed. I'll take it some night when I walk Tuck.*

Another car pulled in behind them, so she told him not to walk her to the lobby. Instead she kissed Bret and waved him off, watching his car meld with the evening traffic. Sara approached her apartment building completely happy. It felt good. As she pulled back the glass door to the lobby, she automatically glanced at the bank of door buzzers. A rose was taped horizontally over the Howells' nameplate.

## Chapter 5

The doorman's desk was empty. Sara looked around for a dropped note. She even opened their mailbox. There was nothing. Only the rose. It was white with a hint of pale pink along the edge of the petals. She held it carefully between the thorns and looked back at the spot where Bret had parked. Surely if he'd had Keesha or Steve leave it for her, he would have said something, or waited for her reaction.

John O'Connor, the doorman, appeared from the hallway as he helped an elderly tenant across the lobby. He shook his head apologetically as she held out the rose and asked who had left it. "I've been away from the lobby for about twenty minutes. Must have just arrived," he said with a wink. "A secret admirer?"

She shuddered. She didn't want any secret admirers — any secrets at all! She turned it slowly between her fingers and sniffed the closed petals. It still smelled fresh. Maybe it was meant for Steve. Maybe things were going well with Marisa Douglas, the administrative nurse he'd been dating. She thanked the doorman and went up to her apartment.

Ten minutes later Steve was circling his heart, the sign for *sorry*. "I don't know any more about it than you do."

Sara signed *M* then made a cross on her upper arm: *HOSPITAL* — their name sign for Marisa. She pulled a bud vase from the kitchen shelf and filled it with water.

"You think Marisa would leave me a flower?" He looked pleased, but as baffled as Sara.

*Call and thank her. See what she says.*

Steve signed *hospital* on his upper arm, but picked up the phone, since she was an administrator in the emergency room and easily reached. Marisa was the perfect explanation, but as Steve spoke to her, Sara read his body language. Even before he hung up, his shrug and the shake of his head told her what she'd expected. Marisa hadn't sent it.

"She says it must be from a secret admirer."

Sara tried to smile. "That's what John O'Connor said, too."

"How about that boy from the regatta you complained about?"

*Maybe. Hope not.*

"Keesha or her parents? They're proud of you."

"They wouldn't leave it downstairs."

Steve agreed, but urged her to cross the hall and ask. They shrugged at each other as Sara picked up the bud vase and left for the Fletcher apartment.

The next morning Sara stood outside the Radley Academy business office and tapped her foot, then checked her watch again. She hadn't expected other students to need the supply room. Now she was sorry she'd waited until the last minute to buy a simple pack of note cards required for her next class.

Keesha had come with her and she, too, tapped her foot. *Can't be late for world history,* she added with her hands.

They were standing behind two ninth-graders who were trying to rush the young clerk as she filled out the purchase forms for a replacement textbook.

"She's going to make me late for math," one said to the other. Sara read their lips and cringed as the harried young woman glared.

"I'm new, okay? You're the one who lost a book," she snapped.

Sara smiled sympathetically. While they waited Keesha signed, *Work/study student from Radley University. Helps Mom's office, too.* She nudged Sara to look at the bulletin board on the wall outside the door. The sports section with the headline DEAF ROWER TRIUMPHS had been posted.

*Your mother brought that in, I'll bet,* Sara signed.

Keesha grinned. Not only was she Sara's closest friend, she was the daughter of the head of the Lower School. *When you decided to leave Edgewood, she's the one who con-*

*vinced the admissions people to accept you.
Now's she the proudest administrator in the
school. Also your proudest neighbor.*

*I know. It's embarrassing.*

"Speaking of our building, did you ever
find out who sent the rose you asked me
about last night?" Keesha added.

Sara shook her head. "I thought it would
be Marisa, the nurse Steve's been dating."

"Not Bret?"

"I called him on the TTY. He says no."

"How about Mike Lenza? He sure paid a
lot of attention to you this weekend. Seemed
like every time I caught a glimpse of him he
was staring at you."

Sara arched her right fingertips into her
left palm. *Say again? Staring at me? Watching?*

Keesha nodded. "You know, at dinner, and
when we were unloading the boats, that kind
of thing. Probably your deafness. It made
him self-conscious, unsure of how to talk to
you."

*All weekend I felt something.* It hadn't
been her imagination. Sara was about to con-

tinue, but the other students finished and there wasn't time. The clerk was glaring at her.

"Sorry," Sara said. "I just need a pack of lined, three-by-five-inch note cards." She spoke as clearly as possible, aware that her muffled speech was difficult to understand.

The young woman frowned and shook her head. In the interest of time, Sara turned to Keesha who repeated it in her clearer voice. "They're right on the second shelf with the pens and pencils."

While the clerk moved to the shelf, Keesha continued. "Let's get back to Mike. He's interested in you. Hot rower."

Sara shrugged it off. "He's not my type."

"Let Liz know. She thought he was great."

Sara signed *L, RED?* the name sign they'd given Liz for her beautiful, flaming hair.

Keesha nodded. "Her crush on Mike Lenza is as big as his crush on you."

*There's no crush. Not on me. I just want him to leave me alone.*

The woman came back with the pack of note cards and handed Sara the student account card already marked: Howell — note cards. Keesha nudged her that the bell had rung.

*She already knew who I was,* Sara signed as they left.

*Get used to it. How many deaf students who make the sports section does this school have?* Keesha replied with a grin.

With the rowing season officially over, Coach Barns reduced practice. Winter sessions would consist of working out and staying in shape, but for now, Sara was looking forward to some free afternoons. Before they were dismissed Monday afternoon, however, the coach surprised them by handing out action shots from the regatta.

Sara added it to the collage inside her locker door. Like many students, her collection consisted of personal snapshots and magazine clippings she was constantly adding to. Kimberly Roth, who modeled after school — and whose magazine ads were on the collage — stopped on her way down the hall to offer Liz, Keesha, and Sara rides home.

"Why don't you hang up your newspaper article?" she asked.

Sara pointed to an ad from the *Gazette* with Kim in it. "One famous student is enough."

*Okay. I'll put your news in my locker.* She laughed as she stumbled over the ASL, but Sara congratulated her on the effort.

Thanks to the ride, Sara was home by 3:45 P.M., in time to find Steve in the kitchen in ratty jeans and a dark sweatshirt. His attire meant only one thing: another undercover assignment.

*Dressed for the docks tonight?* she signed as she dropped her backpack on the table.

He frowned in confusion. *Say again.*

"Undercover?"

*Yes. Sorry. Late hours this week.*

*Be careful.* She wondered if there'd ever come a time when she wouldn't automatically sign the precaution with her heart thumping.

Steve mimed a telephone at his ear. "I got a call from your school. I'm going to chaperon the Harvest Dance."

*You!*

He grinned. "Why not, me? I'm sort of a parent. It might be fun."

Sara arched an eyebrow. "With Marisa?"

"Maybe." His expression grew serious and he gestured toward the table. *Sit down for a minute.*

*Something's happened,* she signed.

He shook his head. "Some questions for you," he said slowly. "I got home a while ago. There was a phone message on the machine. 'What about my chance?' was on the tape." For emphasis, he scribbled it on a piece of paper and handed it to her.

WHAT ABOUT *MY* CHANCE? Sara stared at her brother's note, then shook her head. "Whose voice?" She tapped her throat.

Steve shrugged. "It was growly. Disguised. I couldn't tell if it was a male or a female."

"What about that number you can push — Star 69 — to ring the last call you received? You can find out where it came from."

"I couldn't use it. There was another message after it. Some saleswoman selling carpet." He put aside the making of dinner and came to the table. "Sara, I'm concerned."

*Concerned. Fight with Bret last night?*

*No. Bret's fine. Did the voice mention your name? My name?*

Steve shook his head. *No name.*

*Maybe it was a wrong number.*

Steve left the kitchen. Sara knew even before he returned, that he'd be carrying the rose. He placed the bud vase on the table.

"Somebody left you a rose last night. And today there's a message on the machine in a disguised voice asking for a chance. A chance for what?"

# Chapter 6

Steve slid the vase between them. "If this isn't from Bret, what about that boy — Mike? He followed you home."

*Mike's okay. Persistent. Doesn't give up. Understand?*

*Yes,* Steve signed.

*I told him about Bret.* She tried to ignore the uneasiness creeping into her, the way it had on Saturday.

"He's knows you're not interested." Steve stared at the kitchen counter before he continued. "Maybe he's trying to change your mind. I have a bad week ahead. I don't want to worry about you."

*You don't need to worry!*

*I have to worry!* "Do me a favor. Get in

touch with Mike. Make up some excuse . . . thank him for the rose. See how he reacts. Be nice, but tell him not to leave anonymous messages on the phone. Tell him your brother's a cop and unidentified messages make him nervous."

"He probably was kidding. Just wants me to pay attention." *Wants me to like him.* She put her hand on her brother's arm and got up. "You relax. Worry about your job."

As she left to change out of her school clothes, Steve signed across the room, *You are my job.*

Sara changed into jeans and a heavy shirt and pulled on her thick crew socks. While she was in the closet, she pulled out the dress she wanted to wear to the Harvest Dance. It was a cranberry-colored satin with a scoop neck and long sleeves. The shade complemented her complexion, and with her hair piled into a knot, it was the perfect combination of style and sophistication. And, since she'd only worn it at Edgewood, no one at Radley had seen it. Sara hung the dress on the closet doorknob as a reminder to drop it at the cleaners. She smiled, glad that Bret had talked her into going. It gave her something to concentrate on besides anonymous phone calls.

She wished she could spend the whole afternoon concentrating on the dance and what she'd wear — and Bret. Instead, she grabbed the Radley phone directory and flipped the bulky pages to L. She frowned. There was half a column of LENTZ, quite a few LENZ and even three LENZI. LENZA wasn't listed, not one in the whole area. Maybe she'd misunderstood his name.

Sara opened her closet again and fished through it for her crew jacket. She pulled out the regatta schedule that was still crammed in the pocket. Mike Lenza was printed in the margin. He'd written it to make sure she understood as he tried to introduce himself. Lenza. There was no mistake.

She tried the relay operator and typed in her request for directory assistance. LENZA, Hillsboro. After a brief delay, the message appeared on her screen. No listing by that name in Hillsboro or Radley. Sara thanked the operator and hung up. Alarm had flushed her cheeks and she put her fingers against the unwelcome heat.

She made up an excuse about going shopping and promised Steve she'd be home for dinner.

*No homework?*

*Time for it tonight. I promise.*

Steve waved a wooden spoon at her but smiled as she left. She glanced briefly at the Fletcher apartment door as she waited for the elevator. Keesha would add moral support, maybe even help interpret if Mike couldn't understand her. Then again, there was no guarantee she would even find Mike, nor did she want to embarrass him in front of one of her friends. If he'd sent her the rose and the message, she should handle it privately. She sighed and pushed the button for the basement garage. On the way down she tried to concentrate on getting herself to the Hillsboro boathouse, instead of on the anxiety that kept her cheeks flushed and set her nerves on edge.

Once she crossed the Shadow Point Bridge into Hillsboro, the boathouse was a ten-minute drive south. She found it with no trouble, but when she pulled into the riverside parking lot, there was only a scattering of cars. She parked next to a panel truck as she fought her disappointment. No blue compact. Ridiculous, she chided herself. The Hillsboro team probably followed the same schedule as Radley Academy. There wouldn't be any more rowers here this afternoon than there were at the Shelter Island boathouse.

She searched the lot, then got out of her sedan. With any luck at all, one of the cars belonged to a coach or program director, someone who could give her some information. She shoved her hands into the pockets of her warm-up jacket and lowered her head against the brisk November wind. Her shadow was long, thrust out in front of her by the sun, which was low in the bare-branched trees behind her.

She walked down to the deserted launching area and looked out over the river as she tried to decide how to approach Mike, if and when she found him. She didn't have any experience with demanding boys, especially ones bold enough to leave anonymous messages.

Whitecaps danced on the swells of the

Buckeye River, churned by a passing coal barge out in the middle of the channel. The cold, brittle silence made her shiver. She turned in search of a coach. Lights shone from the administrative and workout rooms. Sara walked back up to the path that stretched from the water around to the main entrance of the boathouse.

As she skirted the building, another long stretch of shadow snaked out in front of her, blending with hers. She turned. Mike Lenza was leaning against the trunk of a maple tree. He had on leather work gloves, a heavy sweater and smudged jeans. He cocked his head and frowned, then smiled coolly as their eyes met. His penetrating gaze startled her.

"Have you been over here watching me?" she said as she reached him.

He knitted his eyebrows. "Watching you?"

She nodded.

He gestured toward the storage bay. "We're putting equipment away for the season. I saw you through the window, but wasn't sure it was you. What a nice surprise."

Sara wished she could read his expression. "I tried to call. No Lenza in the phone book."

He pointed at her, then himself. "You've been trying to find me?" His smile broadened, and he didn't take his eyes from hers.

"There's no Lenza in the phone book. My mother remarried. Robbins is the name in the directory." He took a piece of paper and a pen out of his coat pocket and scribbled his name, address, and phone number. "I guess you don't use the phone. Would I leave a message with your brother, if I called?"

You've already left a message, she wanted to say. Instead Sara made a sign for *phone*. "You can call my TTY through the relay operator, or you can use a TTY. There's one at the Hillsboro library."

"For the public?"

"Yes." *Yes*. Why was she telling him this? "I came to find you, to ask you something important."

"Great." He gave her that cool smile again.

Sara paused before asking, "Did you leave me a rose? At my apartment door? Taped to the buzzer?"

"A rose? No. Somebody brought you flowers?" He avoided her glance.

This was impossible. As hard as she stared at him, she couldn't tell whether his uneasiness was from getting caught because the rose had been from him and he was embarrassed, or because he hadn't thought of it.

She tapped his arm. "Yes. Someone left a rose without a card, just taped to our nameplate in the lobby. Understand?"

He nodded.

"Did you call? Leave a message on the answering machine?"

Mike shook his head. "No message, not from me."

Sara tried to smile. "Okay. Thanks."

"That's it? That's why you came all this way to find me?"

"Yes. And to tell you not to leave messages without your name." She tried to relax. "My brother's a detective. A cop." *Cop*. She scooped her hand forward in the sign. "It makes him nervous."

"A deaf rower with a cop for a brother. You get more interesting by the minute."

Sara read his lips perfectly even though he seemed to be whispering it as an aside. Hearing people never got it. Reading lips was reading lips. Whispering didn't make any difference. She tightened with anger.

Mike looked at her. "Why wouldn't I leave my name?"

Sara shrugged an I-don't-know rather than tell him it seemed like something he might do.

He turned toward the boathouse, then back. "They're calling me. I have to go and help. Sorry I didn't send the rose." His features clouded.

She waved halfheartedly as she returned to her car, uneasy that he stayed where he was and watched until she was out of the parking lot.

Sara returned to Thurston Court with the sun behind the buildings and enough confusion to keep her thinking about every nuance in Mike Lenza's expression. She wasn't convinced he'd been telling the truth, but couldn't come up with a reason for him to lie. The alternative made her just as edgy. If Mike Lenza hadn't left the rose and the message, then who had?

## Chapter 7

"I went to Hillsboro and talked to Mike," Sara said over dinner.

Steve arched his eyebrows from across the table. "Just now in the car? I meant for you to call, not go over there by yourself."

*I was fine. No problem, but he didn't send the rose. Didn't call.*

*You believe him?*

Sara blinked. "I think so. It was hard to tell. Anyway, no harm done."

Her brother nodded and finished dinner lost in thought. *Tomorrow morning. Social worker visit.*

So that's what was on his mind. She patted his arm. Regularly scheduled visits were part of the requirements in order for Steve to serve as her legal guardian. Until she was eighteen there was always a chance that the Department of Youth Services would decide she'd be better off living with their grandparents, or even back at Edgewood.

Sara wanted to tell her brother to relax. Instead she cleared her place and offered to dust the living room and do the week's laundry. Steve slapped his forehead. *Thanks for reminding me. I put a load in while you were out.*

*I'll put it in the dryer when I walk Tuck,* she signed, *and bring it up when we get back.* She patted his arm again. "Tell them you're even chaperoning my school dance. That will get you extra points. I'm hardly out of your sight." She went back to signing. *Life will stay nice and dull this week, you'll see. No excitement.*

*Just a no-name flower,* he signed back, *and a phone call with question voice.*

Despite his struggle with her language, she knew exactly what he was trying to say.

Just a no-name flower — anonymous. Sara

patted Tuck as he trotted toward the laundry room with her. If she had to think about a phone message in a disguised voice while she was in the basement, she needed company. Tuck would have to do. Even though they were in familiar surroundings, the basement was not a place she enjoyed. It was drafty and weird and full of shadows.

Even now when she read a thriller or mystery novel, the Thurston Court basement automatically popped into her head for any setting meant to be ominous or threatening. She gave Tuck another pat as she entered the harshly lit laundry room. One overhead fluorescent bulb was blinking, as if it were fighting to keep its power. The room was empty except for a middle-aged woman who looked vaguely familiar — as many tenants did.

Sara moved the Howell laundry basket Steve had left on top of the third washing machine to indicate which was their load. She dug the wet clothes out of the machine and hauled them across the aisle to the bank of dryers. The lack of vibration on the floor told her that all of the other machines were quiet.

She glanced back at the woman and wondered why she wasn't tending to her own waiting laundry.

Outside the wind was still tossing uncollected leaves, and Sara chose the residential neighborhood one block over for Tuck's walk. On the chilly Radley sidewalks, she decided Mike had been telling the truth. Then, as Tuck nosed the landscaping of the pocket-sized lawns, she changed her mind. Mike had made the call and was embarrassed to admit it.

*What do you think?* she signed to the golden retriever as they waited for the light to change. She shook her head at his eager, brown-eyed gaze. By the time she and Tuck returned to the basement, she threw her hands up in disgust. Be flattered and forget about it, she told herself. The mental Ping-Pong was exhausting.

Sara squinted as she crossed from the dimly lit hallway into the hard fluorescent glow in the empty laundry room. The bulb was still fighting for life, but the woman was gone. Through her sneakers, Sara could feel the floor vibrating. Spin cycle, she thought and put her hand on top of the closest washing machine.

She unclipped Tuck and hung the leash around her neck, then scooped the Howells' fluffed and dried clothes into her basket and left for the seventh floor.

As the elevator door slid open, she nudged Tuck out ahead of her. The building smelled wonderful. It was just after seven o'clock and the aroma of dinner wafted from the apartments. She wondered what the Fletchers were having.

As she made her way down the hall, her footsteps faltered. A bouquet of flowers wrapped in florist's tissue lay on the mat in front of the door to her apartment. She shuddered. Something made her afraid to touch them. She needed a stick, a hanger, something to prod the paper. She pushed them with the toe of her sneaker and finally, heart racing, picked them up. There was no card. She automatically looked around her at the empty hallway.

Inside, she thought. Get inside. Again she looked left, then right, from one end of the hall to the other. There was no motion, no shadows, nothing to break the constant silence. Still she shivered and dropped the arrangement on top of her laundry.

The key took forever to turn in the lock and when she finally got the door open, she closed it behind her and leaned against it as if she were holding back floodwater. Steve had left the foyer lamp on. As always Sara ached for him to be there, the way she still ached for her father. A little detective's common sense would have done her good. She closed her eyes and took deep, even breaths. Steve wasn't there, but neither was anybody else. She worked at convincing herself that she was overreacting.

She snapped on the den light, dropped the laundry basket on the couch, and picked up the bouquet. It was a fall arrangement: besides the mums and carnations there were daisies and greenery. She fingered the florist's tissue. CONNOR'S FLOWERS, City Square ** Hillsboro ** North Haven made a pattern of repeated medallions on the wrapping. Hillsboro. She looked out the window, down into the dark street and empty sidewalks, half expecting to spot Mike Lenza's car at the curb.

Sara came back from the window and stared at the arrangement. She was tempted to drop it in the wastebasket next to the desk, almost as tempted as she was to get back in her car and find the Hillsboro branch of Connor's Flowers. She was sure they would describe the purchaser as a tall, sandy-haired boy about eighteen or nineteen. Then her TTY light flashed, giving her heart another jolt. There couldn't be any growly, disguised voice on this machine, but she was still reluctant to answer it. The blinking light was incessant and she finally lifted the receiver and waited for the typed relay.

**You're home. Sorry I missed you. Did you find the flowers? There's no card because I thought I'd see you.**

**Yes, I found the flowers. You shouldn't have bought them and you shouldn't have brought them all the way over,** Sara typed back.

**That's okay. I should have done it earlier. I wanted to say congratula-**

**tions — for your win Saturday and the article in the paper. Besides, I was in the neighborhood.**

Sara stared at the message and tried to ignore her sense of foreboding. Mike had come all the way into the city with flowers and now he'd found the Hillsboro library's TTY. She regretted ever having told him about it. Why had she done it?

**We need to get some things straight,** he typed.

I drove all the way to the Hillsboro boathouse to get things straight, she wanted to reply. Instead she added, **How did you get in my building?**

**When there was no answer from you, I buzzed Keesha. She let me up. Are you okay? You seem upset.**

Keesha! Now he was calling her best friend, getting himself into the building, and communicating with a telecommunications machine. He was invading too many corners of her life. She typed in her reply. **I am upset. Obviously you lied about the rose. No more flowers! I thought you understood. Just stop! Please.**

Sara, I told you I didn't leave a rose Sunday night. Just the flowers tonight. I stopped by your apartment to ask if you want to double with Keesha and her date for the dance. What is going on with you?

Sara stared at the display board. Who is this? Suddenly, she felt totally confused.

Who is this? It's Bret! Who do you think I am? Sara, who else would give you flowers? What is wrong with you?

## Chapter 8

Sara tried to calm Bret down as she calmed herself. **I'm so sorry. I thought you were somebody else. Please forgive me.** The more she typed, the guiltier she felt. Bret's flowers were beautiful. Innocent. Thoughtful. And she had spoiled the gift.

Bret coolly asked what color her dress was, which finally made her smile.

**Cranberry,** she typed back. **Why?**

Bret replied, **I want to keep Connor's Flowers in business. If somebody's going to shower you with flowers, it better be me.**

Once they signed off, Sara turned back to the silent room. For Bret's own good, she had neglected to tell him about the phone message. What about my chance? Who was it? What did it mean? Bret could be as overly protective as Steve. She'd fought with him about it in the past — but she wanted to avoid it now. She smiled as she placed the flowers in a ceramic container for the middle of the kitchen table.

Despite the fact that she had enough homework to fill up the rest of her evening, she wished night shifts weren't part of her brother's job description. She also wished Bret were just now running an errand in her neighborhood. Nothing would have made her happier than his smiling face at the front door, flowers in hand. With a sigh she turned to the laundry.

She dug through the basket and pulled out her clothes, and began to fold them with distracted glances toward the window. When she'd arranged her own into a neat pile on the couch cushion, she pulled out a crumpled set of Steve's sheets. As she shook out the fitted bottom sheet, she winced as something metal fell on her foot. It was a dog leash, sturdy red nylon with a clip on the end.

She frowned and picked it up. She didn't recognize it. It wasn't Tuck's. She turned it over in her hand. Maybe it was an extra of Tuck's Steve had once bought. She looked at her sleeping dog as if he could explain.

Steve or her father might have used any number of leashes while she was off at school. She put it on top of Steve's laundry and carried the basket into his room, then laid the leash on his bedspread so he'd be sure to see it. With a final shrug, she turned for the homework that would take up the rest of her evening. By the time she got to bed it was after ten. But sleep came slowly.

The harsh blinking of Sara's ceiling light yanked her into consciousness. She propped herself on one elbow as Steve charged across the room. He had the vase of flowers in his hands. It wasn't until he was at the edge of the bed that she focused and realized he also had the leash. His complexion was pale.

"More flowers! Why didn't you call the station?"

Sara sat up, fully awake. *Bret*. "The flowers were from Bret, for my race Saturday and the article in the paper. Not related."

"You're sure?"

*Yes.*

Steve then held out the leash with a questioning glance.

Sara shrugged. "It was in the laundry. Caught in a sheet."

"Washer? Dryer?"

She shrugged again. "I found it in the basket when I started to fold clothes. Old one of Tuck's?"

Steve shook his head.

Sara sat back against the headboard. Steve's hesitant expression was all too familiar. *What is it? What about the leash?* She sat up and stared at him. *What else?*

Steve extended his thumb and pinky from ear to mouth to indicate the phone. He tapped his watch. "There was a message on the machine when I got home. We had a call at ten-forty."

*I was already asleep. What did it say?*

Steve sat on the edge of the bed. "Nothing. It was barking."

"Barking?" *Dog?* she signed, then tapped her throat.

Steve nodded. "A human voice, barking into the receiver."

"What message?"

Steve glanced first at Tuck, curled up at the foot of the bed, then at Sara. His eyes were dark, his mouth a grim line. "No message. Just barking."

"Did you try Star 69?"

"No answer. Just rang and rang." Steve put his hand on Sara's shoulder. "If this doesn't stop, I'll have a tap put in — a tracer. For now, I want you to stay close to home, school, friends. Keep a normal routine. Let me know where you are."

"Do you think this had something to do with the rose? With the other message?"

"Don't know. How well do you know Mike Lenza?"

"Just from the weekend." *Not well,* she added with her hands.

"Stay away from him."

"How would he even know I have a dog? How would he get a leash into our laundry? Why? For what reason?" The answer jolted her into a sitting position. "Am I being followed? Am I being stalked?"

*No!* Steve signed too quickly. His expression wasn't nearly as reassuring as his ASL. "It could be a coincidence. We'll just put the leash in the lost and found corner of the laundry room. I'm sure somebody has missed it. Don't be scared. It won't do any good."

*I'm not scared. I'm angry. I'm fine, Steve. Independent. I don't want some crazy creep to take that away from me. You can't worry. Too much to do in your job, in your own life.* His confused expression made her laugh and she repeated most of it in English. "Understand?"

"I understand somebody wants your attention. Let's hope whoever it is is just going about it the wrong way. Take Tuck to school with you. He's an aid-dog. They're allowed. You know Mrs. Fletcher wants you to show him to the Lower School kids, anyhow. Now might be just the time."

Sara looked at Steve doubtfully. "You think it might help?"

He shrugged. "It'll help me not worry about you so much."

*I'll think about it,* she signed. "Now get some sleep. Tomorrow you have to be perfect for the social worker. We have to show Youth Services that all is perfect here. They have to believe this is where I belong."

Steve nodded. "This is where you belong." *You belong here.*

*Creep or no creep,* she answered.

Steve frowned. He didn't understand, but she didn't repeat it.

Long after he'd gone to his own room, Sara lay awake watching the patterns of light and shadow on her walls. She rolled over. Maybe whoever was doing these things wanted Tuck. She'd heard of dogs being stolen. Of course those were valuable show dogs, worth a lot of money.

Tuck was worth his weight in gold, but only to the Howells and only because of his training as a hearing ear dog and lovable family pet.

Her heart continued its erratic thumping against her ribs. Somebody out there had a plan. Crazy or sane, there was someone in Radley with access to the apartment building who wanted her to know it. She'd watched enough television talk shows to know that stalkers had a logic all their own. Something as simple as friendship or mutual interest could escalate into obsessive need for control. She felt like huddling into a tight little ball and pulling the covers over her head. Instead she lay in the dark room, watching the shadows until she fell back into a fitful sleep. Having Tuck beside her at Radley Academy might be a good idea.

## Chapter 9

At the end of the next day, Sara made her way down the student-filled halls. Passing was made more difficult by the fact that some students were kneeling in front of their lockers to repack their book bags, while others stood and chatted with friends. Most smiled down at Tuck as they rushed to make their buses or were off to after-school clubs or sports.

Student and dog coming through, Sara thought as she wedged herself and Tuck through the small center space. As she worked herself free, the sight at her own locker stopped her. A figure was leaning sideways against the metal with his back to her.

HILLSBORO HIGH SCHOOL was emblazoned across the back of his varsity jacket. It was unmistakably Mike Lenza and he was chatting with Liz Martinson.

As Sara approached, Liz spotted her and spoke to Mike. He turned around and straightened up, arms folded across his chest. Before Sara had a chance to stop her, Liz grabbed her workout clothes and left for the gym.

"Liz said you brought your dog to school."

"Demonstration for the kids. He's an aid-dog."

Mike looked down at Tuck, but it was impossible to tell if he'd understood.

"Why are you here?" she asked after a nod.

"I wanted to see you. Make sure you're all right. I didn't know you brought your dog." His unrelenting gaze unnerved her.

"I'm fine." She opened her locker, which forced him to step aside. "Tuck's good company. He likes it better than sitting around the apartment all day. I can exercise him at lunch."

"Isn't your brother ever home?"

"Yes," she answered quickly. "Mike, I don't have time to talk."

He looked like he hadn't understood. Sara glanced at her fellow students. Everyone seemed to be in the midst of an animated conversation. She could only guess how loud the din was. She pulled her workout clothes from the top shelf.

Mike was intent on the pictures taped up inside her locker. He pointed to a shot of Steve on skis. "Is that the guy you date?"

Sara shook her head. "My brother, Steve."

"The cop?"

Sara's stomach flip-flopped. "Yes, the cop!" She pushed her backpack on top of the extra books in the bottom.

Mike took her by the arm. "Can we talk outside? It's too loud in here. I can't hear you."

*"Too bad you're not deaf,"* she said and signed, but it only added to his confusion. She shook her head. "I can't go outside. Team practice. No time." She tapped her watch and circled her heart. *Sorry.*

"I wanted to know if you've had any more strange messages on your tape machine."

"No," she lied. "Everything's fine." She watched his face, disheartened by his doubtful expression.

"I guess if your brother's a cop, you're pretty safe."

"I'm not in danger."

"You could be. If you don't know who's chasing you."

"Chasing?" She tapped her ear to indicate that she might not have understood.

Mike nodded.

"Why do you think someone is chasing me?" Sara asked, her heart beating quickly now.

Mike shrugged. "I should have said 'interested in you.' Someone trying to get your attention." He glanced over her shoulder, at the wall behind her. She knew without turning around that he was looking at the poster for the Harvest Dance.

Sara tapped her watch a second time. "I've really got to get going." Liz came out of the locker room in her shorts and T-shirt and motioned for Sara to hurry up.

Mike nodded and zipped his jacket. "I don't like it that you can't hear. You'd never know if somebody were sneaking around you. Would you?"

She watched as Mike pulled his car keys from his pocket and walked to the exit.

Liz opened the door of the gym into the weight and workout room. "It's not fair," she said as she looked into Sara's serious expression. "Two great-looking guys are crazy about you. I'm the dance chairman and I don't even have a date."

She was tempted to tell Liz to ask him to the dance. It might help change his focus if another girl showed some interest. However, if Mike Lenza were the source of a barking phone message and disguised voices, she didn't want him anywhere near her and her friends. She stayed silent and followed Liz, grateful for the company of her teammates.

Fifteen minutes later Sara was counting out the rhythm of the workout with everybody else, but her determination did little to relieve her stress. First a flower, then a message, then the barking, and then the leash.

She refused to be helpless and she wasn't about to sit back complacently and wait for something else to happen.

*  *  *

At 4:45 P.M. Coach Barns ended the session with the announcement that they were to do one comfortable jog around the soccer field while there was still daylight.

Sara, with Tuck beside her, fell in behind Keesha and tried to summon the energy to maintain a decent pace. As she glanced across the nearly empty parking lot, brake lights caught her eye at the exit. Mike Lenza's blue compact car was just leaving school property. Shocked, Sara came to an abrupt stop, nearly tripping the runner behind her.

She was still thinking about it as the team left for the night. Mike had been in the building or on the grounds nearly thirty minutes after he'd pretended to leave. With a deep sigh Sara opened her locker and knelt to zip open her backpack. She'd collected the right books for that night's assignments and stood up to grab her jacket.

"Think you'll be adding Mike Lenza to your picture collection?" Liz said as she arrived at the locker.

Sara shook her head and managed a rueful

smile. She frowned. In the left-hand corner, a bare ring of masking tape stuck out where something had been pulled off. She tapped the space as she tried to recall what had been there. Tuck!

She turned to Liz. "Tuck's picture is missing."

## Chapter 10

**L**iz tapped Sara's mouth, her sign that she couldn't understand.

Sara grimaced. She knew she was even harder to understand when she was upset or excited. She pointed to Keesha, who was standing with Kim Roth at the end of the corridor. Liz called both of them over. The minute they arrived, Sara greeted Kim and began to sign and speak so Keesha could translate. *"My picture of Tuck is missing from my locker. Somebody took it!"*

Keesha looked doubtful, but signed and spoke in return. *"When did you miss it? Just now? This afternoon?"*

Sara had to finger spell since she'd hadn't

even given Mike a name sign. *"M-I-K-E L-E-N-Z-A was looking at the pictures, but I don't remember if Tuck's picture was there or not."* She tried to remember the last time she'd noticed it. Last week? Yesterday? This morning? She tapped her temple and shrugged to tell them she couldn't remember. *"Don't know when, but somebody broke into my locker and took Tuck's picture."*

Liz showed Kim where the photo had been. Now that she understood, she put her hand on Sara's arm. "Who'd want a picture of your dog? It probably fell off." She pressed the tape. "Feel. Most of the stickiness is gone. Probably fell off and the janitors swept it up. If it had been lying on the floor, they wouldn't know who it belonged to."

Sara shook her head. *"Somebody broke into my locker."*

Liz pulled Sara's calculator off the top shelf. "To steal a snapshot of a dog, when they could have stolen a good calculator?"

Kim twirled the combination lock. "Do you always lock this? I've seen you open it lots of times without doing the combination. Just like me. Just like Keesha."

Liz grew serious. "If you don't like Mike, then just say so. Lots of other girls would love the attention he's been giving you. I don't want to make you mad, Sara, but don't you think it's kind of stupid to blame somebody like Mike for a missing picture of your dog?"

Sara's cheeks burned. Her flush embarrassed her which only made it worse. She circled her heart. *"Sorry. There's a lot going on in my life."* She tapped the empty space where the photo had been. *"This is just one more thing."*

Kim, Keesha, and Liz waited expectantly for her to continue, but she shook her head in frustration.

It was Liz who finally spoke. "What do you mean?"

Sara sighed. "A lot of weird things have been happening lately."

Keesha frowned. "Sara, you don't think because a picture of Tuck fell off your locker, it's related to somebody leaving you that rose? Relax." *Relax.* "The cleaning crew will be here by the time we finish practice. I'll tell them about it. Maybe they can find it. Was it really that important?"

"What's important," *Important . . .* "is that I don't want anyone in my locker. Privacy." Sara closed her locker, spun the lock, and tried the latch. Her three friends stood around her, but she didn't say anything more. The Youth Services workers were in constant contact with Radley Academy. The last thing they needed to hear was that a rumor was flying through school that Sara Howell was having trouble.

Sara waved good-bye to Keesha as they unlocked their neighboring front doors. The automatic timer had snapped on the foyer lamp, but otherwise Sara entered a dark, empty apartment. Next to the lamp the single pale rose on its tall, thorny stem leaned toward her. She scowled and yanked it from its vase with a cry of pain so loud Tuck turned and looked at her.

"Damn!" she muttered as droplets of blood sprang from her index finger. "Stupid thorns.

Stupid, damn flower." She dropped the rose on the table and sucked her injured finger.

She went into the den and it was a relief to find no blinking message lights on either the regular phone or her TTY. Her finger still throbbed, but the bleeding had stopped by the time she tossed her backpack on her bed. She changed into jeans and an oversized sweater, then grabbed her dress from its hanger and dropped it into a plastic bag.

Keesha had asked her to dinner. Sara and Steve were always welcome at the Fletchers', but Sara turned down the invitation because of the errands she still had to run. Instead of the cozy, home-cooking atmosphere across the hall, Sara wolfed down a microwave pot pie in her silent, empty kitchen. The bright spot was the centerpiece on the table. Bret's flowers had opened into a profusion of fall colors. Not a thorn on any of them, she thought as she ate.

The dry cleaners was up a few blocks on the corner of Penn Street, a ten-minute walk toward the university district. She intended to drop off her dress on the way to the police station. She wasn't looking forward to telling

Steve about the missing photo, but he needed to know. It would also give her a chance to find out how the meeting had gone with the social worker.

She patted her thigh to rouse Tuck. He seemed as reluctant to go out as she did. He'd had his exercise with the crew team.

*Sorry, buddy,* she signed, *but I need company and you're it.* She waited for him to ease out of his prone position, then grabbed her dress. As they left the apartment, she scooped up the rose with the edges of the plastic bag. As she left Thurston Court, she dropped it in the mulch that lay around the boxwood plants in front of the building.

It was early evening and the sidewalks were still full. Commuters spilled from buses; neighbors ran into shops for last-minute errands on their way home. The air smelled vaguely of chocolate from the cookie factory near the precinct station. All of it was comforting. At the dry cleaners Ingrid Hansen, whom Sara had known for years, looked up from her computer and waved.

Sara pulled her dress from the bag and laid

it on the counter, but as Mrs. Hansen was about to take it, she turned to the back room. When she looked back, her expression was apologetic. "Sorry. The sewing machine is jammed." She pointed her thumb toward the seamstress.

Sara shook her head. "Easy order. You go back to your emergency." As soon as Mrs. Hansen nodded gratefully and left, Sara got her pad and paper from her purse and wrote out the simple cleaning instructions. The dance was a week from Friday. Plenty of time to get it back. She grabbed a straight pin from the box on the counter and attached the note on the shoulder. As soon as she finished, she turned with Tuck and headed up Penn Street.

The police station was surrounded by the usual collection of squad cars and although most people wouldn't have found it inviting, Sara entered the reception area happily. Her father, and now Steve, had strong ties to the Fourth Precinct and she was a welcome visitor. A portrait of Detective Paul Howell hung in a place of honor behind the front desk, a touching reminder of how much he'd meant to the force. It was only recently that she'd been able to look at it without tears filling her eyes. It was stressful times like these when she longed for her father's common sense approach. Paul Howell had always had a way of pulling logic from the illogical.

Lieutenant Rosemary Marino, the community liaison officer and friend of the family, was at the desk. *Hi*, she signed in her limited ASL. "Your brother's in his office, buried under paperwork. Go on upstairs."

Sara nodded and took the stairs to the second-floor offices. As Lieutenant Marino had said, Steve was at his desk, which was piled with files.

*Nice surprise*, he signed.

She pulled up a chair. "Social worker." *How was the visit this morning?*

*Good.* "The social worker wants to see you at school, make sure you're —" he fumbled for the word.

"Adjusting? Happy?"

*Yes.*

*School is good. Okay.* "My interpreter, Mrs. Andrews, is perfect for me . . . big help." She lost her train of thought as she looked at Tuck.

"Sara?" Steve waved his hand in front of her eyes.

She sighed. "A picture of Tuck is missing from my locker. I have a collage . . . " She tapped her temple. Did he understand?

*Yes,* Steve signed.

"If it hadn't been for the barking message and the leash, I wouldn't have thought anything about it, but three dog things in two days?"

"You think they're related?"

"I don't want to think they're related. I want to think this is all a stupid coincidence. There's more. Mike Lenza came by my locker after school —"

"The guy from Hillsboro? Sara, I thought we —"

"He surprised me. He said he was worried about me. My locker was open. He was looking at a picture of you. Later, I noticed the picture of Tuck was missing."

*He took it?*

She shrugged.

"Coincidence?"

"I want it to be a coincidence, but I also want you to know what's going on." She leaned back, surprised at the hot tears which gathered on her lashes. The effort it took to stop them made her realize how hard she'd worked at staying stoic. Her friends, her teachers, Bret. . . . They all thought she could handle anything. DEAF ROWER TRIUMPHS. She closed her eyes, but tears squeezed between her lashes. She swiped at them angrily.

Steve leaned over the desk but she waved him back. "I'm okay." *Okay. Really. It's just that I have enough to worry about, to think about. I don't want to worry about Tuck, or you — or me. Why me? Who's doing this?*

# Chapter 11

"**W**hy would someone care so much about dogs?"

Steve seemed reluctant to answer. "Not just any dog. Your dog. It can be part of a pattern." He tapped his temple. "Someone isn't thinking straight. Someone wants your attention and starts out nice, friendly. When you don't respond, he picks something important to you. Again, to get your attention. Don't worry. You probably aren't being stalked, but it could be —"

"Stalked!"

Steve circled his heart. *Sorry. I'm thinking like a cop. Someone just isn't thinking straight.* He began to fumble with his limited

ASL vocabulary and gave up. "What seems logical to them seems crazy to us."

*Crazy?*

*Crazy,* he repeated. "Do you want me to get you a ride home?"

Sara shook her head. *I have Tuck. It's not a long walk.*

*Call me on the TTY when you get back. And Sara, for now, take Tuck to school with you.*

True to her word, Sara called Steve and typed out the message that all was fine in the apartment. She also added that the message light was blinking on his phone. **Can it wait till you get home?**

**That's up to you. Get Keesha to listen to it if it makes you feel better. Otherwise, yes, I'll just pick up the messages when I get back, as usual. Get your homework done!**

**Yes, master,** she typed back, grateful for the humor.

Sara settled in the den with her assignments, a soda and a plate of cheese and crackers. Normally she would have been oblivious to the tiny blinking red light on the phone. She'd always left the messages to her father or brother, but this wasn't a normal night. She was feeling far from normal. She read the same paragraphs three times in her English book before she closed it in disgust and crossed the hall to the Fletchers'.

Keesha answered the door and Sara gave her a sheepish grin and circled her heart. *Sorry. There are phone messages on the machine. Want to come and play them back for me? I can't concentrate on anything with the stupid blinking.*

*This Tuck thing really has you rattled. Are you afraid of what the messages are?*

Sara shrugged. *Not really, just —* she paused, at a loss for words spoken or signed.

"Just antsy," Keesha replied.

Sara frowned.

*Like little ants are running around your shirt.*

Sara laughed. *Antsy.* That was one she needed to add to her vocabulary.

In the Howell apartment, Keesha quickly pushed the replay button on the phone. She listened then pushed the hold button. *Name sign for M-A-R-I-S-A?*

As soon as Keesha finger spelled, Sara replied with *M* plus a cross on her sleeve, the sign for hospital. *M, HOSPITAL means M-A-R-I-S-A D-O-U-G-L-A-S.*

Keesha nodded and repeated it. *Marisa has tickets to a play. Steve should call her tomorrow.*

Sara leaned back in relief as Keesha pushed the button again. This time she frowned, then shrugged as she looked at Sara.

*What is it?*

*The cleaners. It sounds like Mrs. Hansen. She says the tear in your dress is too obvious to repair without it showing. Let her know what you want them to do. They can't guarantee anything, but they're willing to try. She's sorry you didn't show it to her when you were in. It would have saved you time and trouble.*

Sara was on her feet and at the desk before Keesha finished. *What tear?*

*How do I know? The tear on your dress. Hey — what dress?*

As quickly as she could, Sara explained her choice for the Harvest Dance. *Maybe it's someone else's dress she was looking at. It's probably a mistake.*

Although Keesha looked confused, she offered to call the cleaners and straighten out the strange message. Sara shook her head. "Come with me. I have to see the dress myself."

They got to the cleaners within minutes of closing time. Mrs. Hansen came out of the back room with an armload of dirty shirts. She smiled and nodded to both girls and signaled that she'd be right back. When she returned, she had the dress over her arm.

She gave Sara a sympathetic smile as she laid it out on the counter. "I'm sorry I didn't stay at the counter. I could have told you this was too serious to repair."

Sara studied her mouth to make sure she understood every word, then vehemently shook her head. "It was fine when I brought it in."

"Fine! Look at this rip," Mrs. Hansen replied.

*Maybe you caught it on something and*

*didn't know it. A nail in your closet, a zipper?* Keesha signed to Sara with a baffled expression.

Before Sara could respond, Mrs. Hansen laid the tear open. A thin, clean slice ran from the shoulder seam across the front to the waistband.

Sara pointed to the damage as anxiety grew. "This is no tear. This was made by something clean and sharp: a knife, a razor."

Mrs. Hansen's expression changed from confused to shocked. "Who would do something like that? When?" She put her hand to her heart. "Not while I was in the back!"

Sara shrugged that she didn't know. Even Keesha was alarmed. Sara held the dress up to her friend and Mrs. Hansen to prove there was no sign of ragged edges or stray threads that would indicate a tear from a zipper or a hook. She needed information. She needed answers. Sara put the dress down and signed as she spoke. *"I need to find out who did this."*

Mrs. Hansen shook her head. "I hope you don't think this happened here! I told you, I came out from the back room and found it just as you see it. I'm as upset as you are."

Sara pointed to the collar. The pin was still in place, but the slip of paper was missing. *"I left a note with instructions, to make sure you understood."*

Mrs. Hansen shook her head. "I came back out to the counter about five minutes after you left. I picked up the dress. I saw the tear. There was no note. In fact, I went out to the sidewalk to see if you might still be around so I could tell you we couldn't fix the dress. I was sorry I hadn't seen it when you brought it in."

*"You didn't see it when I brought it in because there wasn't any tear then. I left a note on the collar."* She pointed to the pin. *"Someone must have come in after I left, someone who sliced it while you were in the back. You didn't see anyone?"* Sara tapped her ear. *"You didn't hear another customer?"*

Mrs. Hansen looked at Keesha who repeated the question, then hit the keys on her computer and pulled up accounts. She pointed to a suede jacket and the shirts. "Mrs. Parnell, from Thurston Court."

Keesha signed, *Two floor.*

Sara squinted at her friend's shorthand. Keesha meant that Mrs. Parnell lived on the second floor. *"She's a big deal in the Tenants' Organization. Citizens' advocate, that kind of stuff. You know, always has a petition for getting things fixed in the building. Talks to my parents about politics. Nice, I guess,"* Keesha added.

"She came in after you left. She was the only customer before I looked at your dress." Mrs. Hansen waved at the pile of clothes as if she needed to prove that there hadn't been anybody else.

Sara tapped her ear and pointed to the bell. *"Did you hear anything while you were in the back? Even though no one rang the bell for service?"*

"No, but we were running the sewing machine, trying to fix it." She looked at the racks of clothes ready for pickup. "Not one thing is out of place in all those cleaner bags. No one tried to get into the money drawer. The computer is fine." She gave Sara a studied look. "About five years ago I had a teenager in here with a prom dress. She said the dress came in fine, but we found a stain on the front. She accused us of spilling oil on it. Turned out she did it herself because it was a hand-me-down. Her mother wouldn't buy her a new one."

*"Not me! This dress was my favorite, for a dance. You know me. You know my brother. You do all our cleaning."*

"Yes, and I knew your father. If there was no tear in this dress when you brought it in, this is a matter for the police. I can't have vandalism in my store. I can't worry every time I have to turn my back. This is a safe neighborhood. I know all my customers: the Fletchers, the Parnells, the Howells — Why would someone ruin your dress? There are far more expensive things here to steal — or ruin, if that's what someone was after."

The obvious answer stuck in Sara's throat. Nothing else had been touched because nothing else belonged to Sara Howell.

# Chapter 12

Keesha said something and she stopped, then nodded. Mrs. Hansen continued. "I'm doubly sorry if someone deliberately wanted to ruin your dress. I wish I had seen who it was. I wish I could understand why someone would do this."

Sara wanted to add that she felt the same way. Instead, she took the dress and thanked her. *"Please let me know if you think of anything you might have forgotten."*

Mrs. Hansen nodded. "And you'll let me know what happens?"

Sara and Keesha nodded that they would. It didn't help that the proprietor locked the door as they left the shop.

\*　　\*　　\*

*What are you thinking?* Keesha signed as they left.

*Maybe I can find the note that was pinned to my dress. Maybe Steve's department could find a fingerprint on it.* Sara walked silently toward Thurston Court with the ruined dress balled into the crook of her arm.

Keesha tapped her on the shoulder in order to sign. *M-I-K-E. Has he asked you about the dance at school? There's a poster for it right by our lockers. He must have seen it.*

*I haven't said anything. Maybe he thinks I don't go to dances.* She tapped her ear. *No, we haven't talked about it.*

*Does he know about Bret?*

*Yes.* Sara gritted her teeth before she continued. *What are you thinking, that he's so jealous he ruined my dress?* It was important to stay calm, but Sara stopped and hugged herself against the chill. *Why me? Why M-I-K-E? It feels as though someone knows every move I make. Whoever did this followed me here.*

As they walked, Sara had Keesha watch

the street and gutters, desperate for some
sign of the note that had been pinned to the
dress. There was a candy wrapper near the
drain and a few odd scraps but otherwise
the street was clean. Whoever had sliced the
dress had torn the note off, too. In anger? In
frustration? Sara looked both ways along the
sidewalk. Whoever had done it could be with
her right now, one of the pedestrians, someone pretending to shop or stroll along the
sidewalk. Whoever it was had seen her go
into the shop with Tuck. Even if the stalker
hadn't known she had a dog before tonight, it
was a known fact now.

The stalker. She stopped short.

*What is it? Did you find the note?* Keesha
signed.

Sara looked at Keesha and shook her head.
Someone was bent on terrifying her. She
couldn't — wouldn't let that happen. Sara
tapped her arm. *I know you have to get back.
So do I, but come with me to see Mrs. P-A-R-
N-E-L-L. Maybe she saw M-I-K-E — or
somebody else — anybody. Somebody has to
know something.*

Keesha nodded even before Sara finished finger spelling the name.

The Parnells lived in 2C. Same view of the front of the building as our apartment, Sara thought, except much closer to the ground, closer to the coming and going in the guest parking area at the entrance to the building. For the first time all week Sara felt a twinge of encouragement. Even if Mrs. Parnell hadn't seen anything in the dry cleaners' shop, there was a chance she'd glimpsed something outside her own windows: someone arriving with a rose, someone hovering as Sara had left on one of her walks with Tuck.

Another Hansel and Gretel trail, Dad. When Paul Howell had been on a case this thin, he always said he'd searched for a Hansel and Gretel trail. Bits of evidence might be no more than crumbs, but added together, they gave him the leads he needed to solve a case. And now I might be part of a case, Sara added to herself.

Keesha pushed the Parnells' doorbell and smiled reassuringly as they waited. There was barely a pause before the door opened, as if the tenant had seen them enter the building and had been waiting. Sara straightened unconsciously. Mrs. Parnell was the middle-aged woman who had been reading in the laundry room the night before.

The moment their eyes met, Sara's chills returned. Mrs. Parnell studied her, as if her penetrating brown-eyed gaze could lock Sara into her. The glance died, as quickly as it had appeared. She ushered them in, but remained standing in the small foyer.

As Keesha explained the visit, Sara studied the woman's face. Before her father's death, most of Sara's year had been spent away at school and camp. Many neighbors were hardly more than strangers. Mrs. Parnell had probably been around for years in the semi-anonymous way many of the tenants had.

Sara took a breath. Her hearing loss gave her the excuse to study the woman's face as if she were intent on reading her lips as she spoke to Keesha. Her heart thundered in her chest. She wasn't trying to catch every word, she was searching for telltale evidence that this was the person who might shed some light on what was going on. An arched eyebrow, a quick glance at the corner, averting her eyes from Keesha. . . . Sara read seemingly trivial gestures the way a hearing person read words.

Sara ignored her heart as she stared, almost wanting guilt to distort Mrs. Parnell's features. She waited for hot denial, anger — some indication that this woman might be the clue to solving the mystery.

Keesha stopped talking and Mrs. Parnell turned to Sara. Slowly she shook her head. Her look of sympathy seemed sincere. "I walked to the counter and met Mrs. Hansen. There was a crumpled dress . . ." She pointed to the limp fabric in Sara's hand. "It was on the counter."

"Did you see a note pinned to it?" Keesha asked.

The woman shrugged. "No, but I wasn't looking. I was simply dropping off my own things as I usually do."

"Did you notice anyone on the sidewalk watching you or hurrying away . . . anything that would seem suspicious? There was a note pinned to the dress." She waited to make sure she'd been understood. "It's missing. I think whoever cut the dress ripped it off."

Mrs. Parnell looked uncomfortable, then sympathetic. "No. I'm sorry. I can't imagine who would do a thing like this. Have you considered that it might be someone with a complaint against the cleaners? What better way to get back at them than to sabotage another customer, someone who would tell other customers not to patronize them. Word of mouth can be quite effective. I know myself from campaigning in our apartment building to get things attended to." She leaned forward intimately. "Frankly, I'm not always satisfied with that cleaner."

Hearing people. Always whispering. The woman kept turning from Sara to Keesha until Sara lost the gist of the conversation. Her line of reasoning was tough to follow.

Suddenly Mrs. Parnell put her hand on Sara's shoulder. "Of course I know the sadness you've been through, losing your father so recently. You certainly don't need this kind of aggravation. After the funeral, I made the chicken-mushroom casserole. Of course I offered to help your brother when I learned you were coming back to live with him . . . his erratic hours and that dangerous job. . . . It's wonderful that you have Keesha, and that nice young man you've been seeing. I'm sure they're helping with your adjustment. You certainly don't need more aggravation. Aggravation," she repeated when Sara indicated that she hadn't understood.

Sara tried to hide her surprise as her neighbor reeled off her life story. "Do you know Bret?"

Mrs. Parnell looked confused.

Sara spoke slowly. "Bret Sanderson, the boy you just referred to, the one I date."

She shook her head. "No. I've just seen him go in and out of the building with you." She seemed embarrassed. "I don't stare, you understand. It's just —" She shrugged and gestured vaguely toward the living room window behind her. " It's all right out there."

"What is?"

"Life." She raised her chin. "Life."

As she gestured Sara glanced into the living room. Even as darkness fell, she had the shades open. It was easy to see the bright glow of the parking lot lights.

"Mrs. Parnell, have you ever noticed anyone following me recently, like when I walk my dog, Tuck?"

The woman cocked her head as she strained to understand. "Walked your dog?" She grimaced. "I don't like dogs, especially big ones like that retriever of yours. No need in the city, in the building . . ."

"Tuck is trained to help me," Sara said simply.

" . . . threatening. Dogs that size. Even last night in the laundry room . . . too big."

Sara swallowed slowly. She'd come to ask for help, help from a woman who had been the next customer in the dry cleaners and who was now frankly admitting to disliking Tuck.

## Chapter 13

A few years earlier, her father had written to her at Edgewood about someone circulating a petition to prohibit pets in the building. Even if it had gone through, Tuck, as an aid-dog, would have been excluded. Still, Paul Howell had written that he and Steve, the Fletchers, and many others had no complaints about how the tenants handled their pets. The petition had failed. She tried to remember if her father had said the petition had been circulated by a Mrs. Parnell.

Sara gasped, unaware that she'd made any noise until Mrs. Parnell and Keesha looked at her. She rubbed her suddenly sweaty palms against her jeans. Calm down. Steve must run into this kind of thing every day. Police work was full of trails that lead to fake conclusions, sudden suspicions of innocent people.

She wished her brother hadn't explained that stalkers could be seemingly normal people. This seemingly normal woman in front of her was adding that if Sara had been with Tuck right now, she wouldn't have let her into the apartment. Sara calmed herself. Okay, so she'd be left out in the hall. Fear of dogs wasn't necessarily the same thing as hatred of dogs, and just because a leash had shown up in the laundry, it didn't mean . . . what? That this mild-mannered, middle-aged apartment activist was crazy? Was out to get her? Had taken a snapshot out of her locker? Had followed her to the cleaners with a razor and slashed her dress for the Harvest Dance? Mrs. Parnell?

Anxiety wouldn't do a thing but add to her confusion, but Sara was helpless to stop the sudden pounding of her heart. It made her lightheaded as she signed *Thank you for your information.*

Mrs. Parnell looked to Keesha for an explanation. "Thank you," Keesha reiterated.

"If you think of anything else that might help, let us know."

"Certainly." Mrs. Parnell looked at Sara. "You stay close to that brother of yours. I know he often works at night. It must be just awful up there all by yourself, so soon after the loss of your father. You're certainly welcome to come down here and visit with me when you need company. Just leave your dog at home."

Sara's stomach tightened. Her ears burned as shock drove a flush across her cheeks. Steve's schedule; her hours alone. . . . This woman chatted as if they were family friends. Sara managed to thank her, all the while burning to know how she got her information.

*Friend of your mother's or busybody,* Sara signed to Keesha as they left the apartment and stepped back into the hall.

Keesha shrugged. *I'll ask Mom. She's right, you know. You need company.*

*Not her company.*

Keesha hooked her index fingers. *Friends.* It was the name sign they had used for each other for ten years.

Sara smiled gratefully. *You know I'd be at your place in a second if I ever felt really threatened.*

Sara had intended to ride the elevator back up with Keesha, who was already complaining of her waiting homework, but also demanding that Sara stay at the Fletchers' until Steve got home. Sara shook her head. *Thank you, but I can't give into this. Steve won't be too late. Go on up. I want to check on something first.*

*What?* Keesha looked skeptical.

*Outside. I want to go out and see what P-A-R-N-E-L-L-S' view is. So I can kiss Bret where she can see it. Go on up. The doorman is right there.*

*You'll be okay?* Keesha asked as she stopped laughing.

Sara nodded and nudged her friend toward the elevator. She took the fire stairs one flight down to the lobby. As she crossed it, John O'Connor flagged her down and handed her a note. Sara was tempted to tell him to keep it. Whoopee, another ploy to terrorize me.

She flipped the folded paper open gingerly, as if it might explode.

> Sara,
> You must be out. I was on my way home from the library and stopped to see if I could talk you into a quick study break. A cup of coffee at the Side Door Café, or something. Just as well. MAJOR Latin test tomorrow. Call me later.
>
> Bret

Nothing would have cheered her more than time with Bret, even something as quick as running into a local coffee shop. She stuffed his note in her jeans and hurried outside, anxious to finish her sleuthing and get upstairs to her TTY.

The blast of night air felt good after the suffocating events. Sara hoped she looked nonchalant as she strolled out along the brick walk to the small parking area. It was reserved for visitors and required a pass which the doorman issued. She walked to the curb and looked back at the building, at the Parnell apartment. She recognized the outline of the swag draperies at the double living room window from what she'd glimpsed inside. She wondered if Mrs. Parnell had a favorite chair and a pair of binoculars. Sara grinned to chase the mood. She and Bret could give her something to stare at.

Even thoughts of Bret did little to keep Sara's mind from racing back to everything that had happened, everything that was piling up like unsolved police files. She still had the torn dress in her arm. Was someone watching now? Someone across the street? Someone in a parked car? She looked back at Thurston Court. Someone in her own building?

Unwanted tears squeezed from her eyes. She pretended to rub them. No one could see her cry. Why would anyone want to bother her? What had she done? Or was it something she hadn't done? Sara stood at the curb and looked at Thurston Court.

All her life this building had been home, a fortress against the tragedy in her life, a safe haven. Now somebody was trying to destroy all that, someone who knew more and more about her habits and her schedule.

She looked again at the windows of 2C. It was Wednesday night. In four short days her life had been deliberately turned upside down. And who do I suspect: a middle-aged woman, and a teenage athlete. Of course that means Mrs. Parnell would sneak into Radley Academy, and steal a snapshot of Tuck from my locker. That's about as logical as presuming Mike Lenza had snuck into the Thurston Court laundry room and left a leash in the dryer. She shook her head and started back across the street. She was the daughter of a detective, the sister of one. She tried to imagine what Steve would pull from these eerie episodes. Could he tie them together or would he attribute some to coincidence? At first glance it seemed ludicrous that two people as different as Mrs. Parnell and Mike Lenza could be suspected of the same thing. As hard as it was to admit, there was one common denominator: Sara.

The rose had started it all. She shouldn't have been so quick to get rid of what she now thought of as evidence. Gingerly, she stepped to the walkway and leaned over the spot where she'd dropped it into the mulch. It was nearly hidden by the prickly leaves of the holly bush. Now, however, the thorny stem of the faded white rose was encircled by the note she'd pinned to her dress in the cleaners.

## Chapter 14

The tears she'd managed to wipe away sprang back, hot and fresh. Sara spun around with a force that nearly tumbled her into the bushes. There was no one lurking at the curb, or ducking behind a parked car. It was the same clear, breezy night she'd walked Tuck in, visited Steve, stopped at the dry cleaners. Met Mrs. Parnell.

Sara looked up at the second floor, then stared at the rose. She wanted to grind it all under her heel, the flower, the note, the fear. She suddenly felt nauseous and shaky. She fought for common sense.

As she pulled the paper from around the thorn she snagged her finger for the second time that night. The prick of pain made her wince, but the pain went much deeper than her finger. Who are you? The silence was broken only by the pounding in her head. Someone was watching.

Someone watched me leave the building the first time with Tuck; someone watched me toss the rose into the bushes. Whoever it was followed me to the cleaners, slit the dress and tore off the note, then wrapped it around the rose. Why?

Sara tried to think like someone obsessed. The rose was exactly where she'd left it. The stalker had either taken it and brought it back, or stood where she was long enough to wrap the note so tightly the thorns stuck through. Why go to all that trouble for something that was just going to lie in the landscaping?

Sara knew the answer the minute she started for the entrance. The stalker knew she'd regret throwing away the rose, that she'd go back for it, that she'd find one more piece of evidence that her life was under a microscope. Evidence. This was also evidence for the police. She took long steadying breaths before finally entering the building with the flower, the note, and the ruined dress.

John O'Connor held the door for her, but shook his head when she asked of he'd seen anyone near the bushes. His desk and telephone were inside the entrance, out of sight of that part of the parking lot. She also asked as clearly as possible who had come in and out within the last hour and got the answer she had suspected. He recalled Mrs. Parnell, Keesha and herself, and half a dozen other tenants. He added Bret. The few guests he didn't know had been accounted for.

If someone as unsuspicious as Mrs. Parnell had picked up the rose, it wouldn't have aroused any suspicion. She grimaced at the irony. Bizarre incidents were calculated to terrify her, yet by themselves, each one was hardly more than an odd occurrence, easily undetected. It was a long ride up the seven flights to her apartment.

Marcus Fletcher was in the hall. Keesha's older brother was heading toward the incinerator room with a bag of cans to be recycled. Sara tapped her mouth to indicate she had a question.

"Do you know who Mrs. Parnell is? The woman in Two-C?" She held up two fingers and added *C*.

"Busybody," he replied.

"Yes. Crazy question, but would she ever come to school, to see your mother or something?"

Marcus didn't even look surprised. "Sure." *Yes.* After years of knowing Keesha's best friend, Marcus answered Sara in a combination of slow, distinct English and bits of ASL she could understand. "Mrs. Parnell thinks of herself as a political activist. *She works with the World Affairs Club sometimes.* You know, on human rights issues, petitions to stop killing whales. She's always giving me some poster or notice to put on the student government bulletin board outside the auditorium."

Sara could feel the blood drain from her face as she read his lips. Years of practice with Marcus made it easy, but she wished she'd misread what he was implying. Mrs. Parnell could have been in the school corridors, the same way she could have quickly knelt at the holly bush. No one would have questioned it.

She thanked Marcus. *I was just curious about a neighbor.*

"No problem," he replied. He continued down the hall to the common room where tenants disposed of their trash and left newspapers, plastic, and glass for recycling. Sara unlocked her front door. Steve was due home in less than an hour. She needed her brother as soon as possible.

Once Steve got home, he used his pocketknife to point at the tear in her dress. He'd laid it out on the kitchen table and under the direct light of a small flashlight, he confirmed what she'd told him. It was a clean, deliberate slice from a knife or razor. No accidental pull or catch of the fabric had ruined it. "A restraining order can help in cases like this, but in order to do that we need a name, a person, proof of who the suspect is, not just what he or she is doing."

Sara slammed her fist on the table. *He or she is driving me crazy! I hate this. Who? Why?* "So far the only people I suspect are the same ones that have been concerned. Mike —" *M-I-K-E.* "He says he came to school to make sure I was okay after I told him about the rose and the first phone call. He said he was glad you were a cop." That, at least, made her grin. *So am I.*

"Mrs. Parnell. We hoped she knew something, saw someone at the shop. She got all motherly over my being alone. Wants me to come stay with her in the evening." She shuddered. "She knew so much about you and me it gave me the creeps —"

Sara pointed to her dress. "She suggested someone was mad at the cleaners. Someone slashed the dress to get them to lose customers. That could be it, Steve. Maybe this has nothing to do with me. Nothing to do with the leash or the barking — or anything." She tapped her forehead and brought her hand forward in a hard, quick, angry motion. *Don't know. Don't know anything anymore.*

"Until we have a suspect and can get a restraining order, I want you to change your routine. Different ways to school and back. Let the doorman or me walk Tuck, or if you do, take Keesha or Marcus with you and use a different route. Don't go alone."

She stuffed her hands into her pockets. "You sure don't have to worry about that."

She pulled out Bret's note, anxious to get to her TTY.

"What's that?"

She showed him. "A note from Bret. He stopped by before you got home. I was at Mrs. Parnell's."

"He was here tonight? He could have seen you leave for the cleaners?"

Sara stiffened. "John O'Connor said he came by. If Bret had seen me, he would have caught up with me."

Steve didn't reply. The look on his face made her furious.

Steve scooped the dress up from the table. "I know this will be tough, but for the time being I don't want you to talk to anybody about stalkers. Let your friends think whatever problems you had are over." He slid the dress to the crook of his arm and rotated his open fingers at the wrist. He signed, *Finished.* "Tell Keesha you agree with what Mrs. Parnell suggested. You can say I discovered that someone's angry at the dry cleaners."

*I can't tell Keesha?*

He shook his head. "I don't want rumors around that might scare away the stalker."

"Or make him more desperate? Is that what you really mean?"

Steve nodded slowly. His handsome features were drawn. *Yes.* "That's what I really mean. We don't know who, or what, we're dealing with yet. Trust me on this, Sara."

She knew she was reading the lips of a concerned detective, not her brother. *What about Bret? He doesn't even go to my school, doesn't see anybody. Bret wouldn't tell.*

"Especially not Bret."

*Not Bret!* She punched the air as her hands spoke. "I have a date for his game Friday, and the dance is next weekend. If I have to break things off, he'll want to know why. It will make things worse, not better."

Steve circled his heart. *I'm sorry.* "He was here tonight. He could have set this up as easily as the other two. He could have left the rose, then sent more flowers to throw you off. You two have had plenty of disagreements in the past. Go to the game, but I'll go, too. That's the only way. I've wanted to see him play, anyway." *I hate this, too.*

*Then be fair.*

Steve scowled. "Fair! Bret was here tonight. He was here Sunday night."

*That's not fair!*

"Sara! Nothing about stalkers is fair. They thrive on the unexpected. The rose, the phone call . . . I'm sorry, really, but he knows enough already."

"But I need my friends."

Steve gave her a studied look that sent chills into her scalp. "You've watched talk shows. You've read articles. Whoever is tormenting you could very well be one of your friends."

## Chapter 15

The change in Sara's routine started first thing in the morning. Despite her protests and his lack of sleep, Steve got up and drove her to school. She thanked her brother half-heartedly as he pulled their green sedan into the Radley Academy parking lot. Part of her was glad to have the support, but it was also a reminder of how serious the situation had become.

As she reached for her backpack, Steve put his hand on her arm. "Don't be surprised if you see Lieutenant Marino on campus," he said.

"Because she's doing another drug awareness program, or because you think she can help?"

*Help*, he signed. "It's the perfect setup. She works with schools and kids half the time anyway. I'd feel a lot better if we had somebody in there with you."

"Even she can't just walk into the building without signing in."

Steve turned off the ignition. "Leave that up to me. Once I get you inside —"

*No way! You're not going to walk me into school every morning! I've got Tuck the attack dog.*

Steve laughed. "Tuck the fur ball is more like it. I can always tell when you're really angry. You automatically start to sign, even if I can't understand a word."

"I don't need —"

"Calm down. I'm going inside to make an appointment at the business office. Scott Hardesty handles security. He can approve Rosemary's visits."

"The business manager? He's the one who lost my permission slips for the regatta."

"Dad worked with him. Brenda Fletcher had Dad talk with him last year about security. You were away at school, of course."

Remnants of grief made her sigh. Steve

lost his focus for a moment and stared through the windshield. Neither would have ever guessed at the changes one year could bring. Sara put her hand on his arm and he turned back to her. He circled his heart.

Sara circled hers. *I miss Dad like crazy. I'm sorry, too. Go on in. I'll walk Tuck and get to homeroom.*

*Careful,* he signed. "Call when you get home after school. I'll be at the station or they can page me."

Sara thanked him, grabbed her backpack, and slid from the car. She eased Tuck from the backseat and joined the bustle of arriving students, knowing full well that after Steve collected his thoughts, he'd hang around the entrance long enough to observe the comings and goings on campus.

Change your routine. Don't leave yourself vulnerable. Stay safe. She was part of a game, a sick game she had to play by someone else's rules. By midmorning she had added her own directive: Reason like someone who doesn't think straight.

There wasn't much she could do to alter her school routine, but with Mrs. Andrews, her interpreter, sitting next to her in nearly every class, and Tuck with her even in study halls, she felt safe enough to concentrate on what her teachers were trying to accomplish.

English class came and went, then history, then her computer lab. Like every other student her class schedule was on file in the office. Until this week she'd never given a thought to who might want to know whether she had biology 1 at ten in the morning or contemporary European history.

Reason like someone who doesn't think straight. Fourth period she asked for a pass in study hall to use the library. She set her books in a study carrel along the far wall past the reference section.

Each desk had an eighteen-inch partition around it for privacy and concentration. Ideal, she thought as she propped open her biology book. She glanced at her notes from Mr. Hagstrom's class, then turned the notebook to a blank piece of paper. She had forty-five minutes of uninterrupted time to figure out what five days of unrelated clues had in common besides Sara Howell as victim. She counted the days on her fingers. Four days, actually. It was Thursday morning and nothing had happened. Yet.

Sara drummed her fingers on the desk and stared at the blank wooden partitions that formed her cell. Her shoulders tingled as if she were about to be touched. Or grabbed, or yanked backward out of her chair. Sara! She felt foolish, like a child engrossed in a thriller who's suddenly tapped by a playmate. She sucked in a deep breath and tried to focus on the blank notebook page in front of her. She slid her foot to the right until she could feel Tuck's even breathing. What did a deliberately slashed dress have to do with a leash in the dryer, a bark on the answering machine? A creeping sensation started up her spine and worked its way into her scalp.

It wasn't the silence. She lived in a silent world. It was the tan, polyurethaned, wooden panels that surrounded her. Like blinders on a skittish horse, they kept out visual stimulation. Without hearing, it was visual stimulation that kept her grounded. The panels might as well have been a blindfold. She was skittish enough. This made her feel as though the next terror-inducing prank was about to occur directly behind her. When she couldn't stand it any longer, she spun around in her chair. The librarian was straightening a set of encyclopedias.

Less than five minutes after she'd laid out her books, Sara scooped them into her arms and crossed the library to the round tables already peppered with students working on research papers. She needed more than canine company. A freshman smiled at her as she set down her books. Company. Sara's pulse slowed.

Twenty minutes later she leaned over her notebook and stared at the list she'd devised. Her pulse was back to its pounding.

Rose * Tape: Chance * Tuck's photo * Leash * Tape: Barking * Dress

1. Mike Lenza
   a. wants to date me
   b. insistent

2. Mrs. Parnell
   a. hates dogs

>    b. tried to help when Dad died
>    c. busybody
>
> Both:  a. access to school
>       b. access to apt. building
>       c. too much interest in me

One name was conspicuously absent. She couldn't bring herself to add Bret Sanderson to the chart. In the two months she'd known Bret, they'd had arguments serious enough to stop dating, but nothing about him had ever given her the slightest indication that he might be capable of what she was dealing with now.

Maybe the stalker had picked her at random. Phone messages could easily indicate that the stalker didn't even know she was deaf. Maybe Mrs. Parnell had been right about someone disgruntled with the cleaners. The dress incident could be unrelated to the rest. The leash could have been a truly lost article in the dryer. The rose and the first message could have been from Mike Lenza, too embarrassed to admit he'd had a crush on her. The snapshot of Tuck could easily have fallen out of her locker. Couldn't it be that everything just seemed sinister when it was all added together? Couldn't it be that things were fine? Starting today, life could return to normal. Couldn't it?

Sara leaned back in her chair. The library was comfortable, warm, brightly lit. No one was staring or threatening or plotting. Maybe she was imagining all of it. Maybe.

She drew circles in the margin and loops across the bottom of the page. The pencil felt like the indicator on a Ouija board, as if she held it long enough Bret Sanderson would appear on the page without her having to write it.

She propped her chin in her hand. All the Rosemary Marinos in the precinct weren't going to do a scrap of good if she pretended life was normal, if she couldn't help them with motives, or names, or at least suspicions of what the stalker might be after. Sara stared at her chart and thought of her father. Lieutenant Paul Howell would have told her what Steve was trying to make her understand: She had to think like a cop, not a victim.

Her heart ached. With the exception of Keesha, Bret was the only friend who knew where the laundry room was. More than once he'd been in the dungeonlike basement when they'd gone biking together and brought the bikes in so they wouldn't get stolen. Bret could have dropped off the second arrangement of flowers to appear innocent, the same way he might use the normal phone rather than the TTY. That's what a cop would say. Bret knew Tuck. No one would question him at her locker. He could have been there while she was at crew practice. Bret was the only one who knew she'd picked a dress for the dance. And that she intended to take it to the cleaners when she walked Tuck. Because he'd told her to take it. Had he waited and watched?

Is this what it feels like to be crazy? To suspect the people closest to you? To find evil where you thought there was only good? Hot, unwanted tears blurred her vision. Students suddenly moved, stretched, gathered books. Sara pressed her hand to her eyes, then glanced at the clock. Obviously the bell had rung. She moved the pencil from the margin and slowly added one final name to her chart: Bret Sanderson.

## Chapter 16

The minute last period finished, Sara headed for her locker. She couldn't wait to get out of the building. Whether Steve was home or not, she wanted to be in Thurston Court with her dog, her homework, anything to divert her attention.

Every time she'd rounded a bend in the corridor or changed floors, she'd half expected to spot Mrs. Parnell at the end of the hall, or at the top of the stairwell. It was a small relief that by three o'clock there was no sign of the woman. There hadn't been any sign of Lieutenant Marino, either.

As Sara headed for her locker, it was Kimberly Roth who waved from the end of the hall. Despite the bustle of students, the pretty blonde stood on tiptoes and signed *K, CAM-ERA*, the name sign they'd thought up recently because she modeled professionally. Next she pantomimed driving a car, their sign for the offer of a ride home.

*Yes. Thanks. Let me get my books,* she signed back.

Kim grinned. *I have to go to the office first. Ready in ten minutes.*

*Okay. Ten minutes. Tuck and I will be out at your car.* It lightened Sara's mood to see Kim's grin. Fifty feet away with scores of kids making who-knew-how-much noise, Sara had understood perfectly. Her hearing friends were discovering what Sara had known for years. There were advantages to a language that was spoken with hands.

The smile on her face lingered, then disappeared. She nearly bumped into Mike Lenza, who had materialized once again.

"Hi," he said as he stepped closer.

Her heart charged into its familiar overdrive as it lurched and thumped against her ribs. She nodded in return and tried the latch on her locker. It was locked. As unobtrusively as possible, she blocked his view and worked the combination. When it opened, she dropped her backpack and finally turned to face him. He was looking from Tuck to the pictures.

*Sorry,* she signed. "I'm in kind of a hurry. I have a friend waiting."

Mike nodded. "My coach sent me over to pick up the VCR tapes of the regatta your coach borrowed. Since I'm here —" he jammed his hands in his pockets, then pulled them out, "I've thought about calling you with that relay operator, or whatever, but it would feel really strange asking you out through somebody else."

"Asking me out?"

He shrugged and glanced at the dance poster as he had on Monday. "Next Saturday. Let's do something."

*Sorry.* "I'm busy." She followed his glance to the poster.

Mike looked surprised and vaguely uncomfortable. "I thought you might be free since . . ." He shrugged and shifted from one foot to the other. ". . . you know."

She tapped her ear. "I'm deaf?"

"Right."

"I dance. And I'm dating someone, remember?"

His face darkened as a flush crept up from his collar. "Yeah, I remember."

She circled her heart again. "You'd better find Coach Barns before she leaves."

Mike nodded. "Can you show me how to find her?"

The gym was on her way out of the building anyway. She grabbed her backpack. She and Tuck led Mike down the hall and into the gym office.

Sara leaned back as Kim pulled her car from the campus parking lot. Since communicating was impossible while Kim watched the road, Sara looked at the new tapes Kim had balanced on the cup container on the console between their seats. One of the first things she'd explained to these new, hearing friends was that she, too, was interested in rock bands.

As Kim pulled the car up to the entrance of Thurston Court, Sara signed, *Great group*. "Keesha just bought this one, too."

Kim nodded. "I'd love to see them in concert."

Sara thanked her for the ride, and opened the console between the bucket seats where Kim kept the rest of her music. At the same moment that she picked up a folded piece of newspaper that lay on top of the tapes, Kim flipped the console cover back down on her hand.

"Sorry," Kim was saying. "Sorry, Sara, really. I didn't want you to see it."

Sara frowned as she tried to read Kim's lips. "See what?"

Kim's usually flawless complexion was mottled in embarrassment. Gently she tugged the newspaper from Sara's hand.

"It's nothing. Somebody was probably just fooling around while they waited for a ride or something."

Sara frowned again, unable to make sense of Kim's speech. *Say again.* She gave her the sign to repeat herself.

Kim shook her head slowly.

Sara tapped her temple. "Kim, I don't understand."

"The article from Sunday's paper about

you. I brought it to school to tape in my locker, but didn't remember till this afternoon. I put it on top of my books just now when you said you'd like a ride home, but when I came back from the office, it was — somebody had — I should have thrown it away before I got in the car. *I'm sorry.*" She circled her heart as Sara had taught her. "It was probably just some dumb kid in the hall killing time."

The moment Kim stopped talking, Sara looked at the crumpled newspaper. It had been punched full of small holes. Her stomach knotted. "You weren't going to tell me about this?"

"Heck, no. You know what? I bet somebody was hanging around, talking to friends. . . . You know, like doodling when you talk on the phone. Somebody just punched holes in this while he or she talked." Kim smiled, but it seemed to take an immense amount of effort. "Even if this were done on purpose, what do I care if somebody doesn't like you? Plenty of kids think I'm a snob. Whoever it is, is just jealous."

"Did you see who did it? Do you have any idea?"

Kim shook her head. "When I came back from the office, it was just sitting on top of my backpack."

Get your heart back in your chest. Sara took small, even breaths. "Thanks for trying to help. Don't worry. I'm not hurt," she managed as her throat closed. "I'll throw it out." Her smile felt stretched, glued to her teeth and she hoped she didn't look as frozen and paralyzed as she felt. She and Tuck got out of the car.

The minute Kim pulled away from the apartment, Sara scoured the street for something — anything — suspicious. Most of all she looked for Mike Lenza's car. There was nothing to make her think she'd been followed. There never was. She ignored John O'Connor and rushed for the elevator. Once inside she hit 7 and leaned back against the wall. In the privacy of the brightly lit cubicle, she took a closer look at the remains of the *Gazette* article. It had been punched full of tiny holes. Many were in the middle of her smiling face.

## Chapter 17

Kim hadn't planned on telling her. Kim wanted to spare her feelings. Sara opened her empty apartment with shaking fingers and wondered how many other episodes her friends were keeping from her. Evidence. She dropped her backpack in the foyer, but ran down the hall to her room with the clipping.

She yanked a box from the bottom of her closet and emptied it onto the floor. The box might not even hold all the evidence that was piling up. She carried it into her brother's room. The leash, the rose, and the note were on Steve's desk. She put them all in the box with the article, like odd treasures from childhood.

*I won't give in to this. I won't.* Sara signed to herself. She'd changed from her school uniform into jeans and a turtleneck. She rifled through her backpack on the kitchen table and pulled out the list she'd made in study hall. She focused on the name she'd added so reluctantly at the end of the period. "Bret Sanderson" had been scrawled at the bottom of the page. With a satisfied grin she drew a line through his name.

Her tormentor had been at school this afternoon; she had the proof in the box. Whoever had punched holes in the article had been in the Radley Academy building less than half an hour ago. Since she'd met Bret she'd teased him about going to a rival school. Thank you Mr. and Mrs. Sanderson for sending him across town. She relished the flood of relief that washed through her. She might not know who the stalker was, but at least she knew it wasn't Bret.

She ruffled Tuck's fur and buried her face in his neck. *Sorry buddy. I know we just got home, but we're going back to school,* she signed. When she'd pulled on her crew jacket, she snapped Tuck into his leash. *It isn't Bret,* she signed as they rode the elevator to the dingy basement. Tuck looked at her with the same curious brown-eyed stare he always had. His gentle panting made her grin. Or maybe it was relief. She hugged herself until the elevator stopped, then led her retriever through the hallway to the entrance to the garage. It isn't Bret, Sara thought to herself.

The parking lot of Radley Academy had thinned out in the half hour since Kim had driven Sara home. She pulled into an empty spot. Not being able to tell Kim what had been going on for the past week had cost her precious time. Kim was a loyal friend who would have turned her car around and hightailed it back before the perpetrator had a chance to leave the building.

Perpetrator. Perp her father had written on a piece of paper the summer she'd tried to decipher what he and Steve were talking about as they discussed one of his cases. Now there was a perp in her life, a threat to everything she'd worked so hard to accomplish since her return to Radley. She was tired of the terror and the anxiety. Maybe if she got angry enough . . . maybe anger would keep her levelheaded. She switched off the ignition. It was anger she'd use to keep herself focused. Whoever was doing this had no right to invade her life.

*Guard dog,* she signed to Tuck as he jumped from the backseat onto the pavement. She wished she knew who he was guarding ~~her~~ from. Once she was inside, she took a deep breath and gathered her thoughts. Somebody had to have seen something.

Sara was hardly through the door when three Lower School kids who barely came up to Sara's waist buried themselves in Tuck's fur and hugged him around the neck. Aid-dogs weren't to be handled. She knelt and tried to explain while she fought her impatience. They were taking up precious time.

"What's wrong with your voice?" the smallest asked.

"She's the rower with broken ears, stupid," the second one said as she elbowed her buddy. They looked back at Sara curiously. "Mrs. Fletcher told us about you and your dog. We saw you in Mrs. Gray's class. She said you might bring him to ours."

"I might," Sara replied. For good measure she signed, *good-bye, see you later.*

The brunette pointed down the hall. "You're on the bulletin board at the other end of the building."

Sara smiled. "I know. Thank you." *Thank you.*

Both kids copied her and as she left, they were still experimenting with the signs.

The bulletin board. Just glancing in that direction made her heart race, but she had work to do here first. With Tuck beside her she scoured the hall and then the gym. Thursday afternoon. Upper School girls' basketball practice. She watched the chaos of drills and felt the thunder in her feet. She had no idea what she was looking for: a glare? A fake smile to tip her off? She knew even as she turned to leave there wouldn't be anything that obvious.

Whoever was after her wanted it that way,

wanted her tormented, confused. There'd been no overt threat on her or her safety, just eerie, sporadic episodes to throw her off balance. Terrify her was more like it, she thought, as she and Tuck walked up and down the narrow aisles between the lockers in the changing area.

She couldn't enter the boys' locker room. Their practice started after the girls', and some were arriving as she turned the corner. One nodded, another grinned. There was nothing sinister or suspicious. Mike Lenza filled that category all by himself.

Sara stood at Kim's locker and imagined she were Mike. She walked through the conversation with him, the episode at her locker. Would he have had time to deface the article? She knew the answer before she finished asking herself. Sure.

Mike wouldn't have known Kim meant to stick it in her locker. If Mike had seen Kim put it down on top of her backpack it would have been logical to guess that she'd meant to give it to her. If he'd knelt on the floor or squatted as if he were tying his laces or checking for something, it would have been easy to jab a pin or pencil point through the article. If, if, if.

Sara tugged Tuck's leash and reminded herself of why she'd come back. They hurried toward the bulletin board outside the business office. She envisioned pinholes and punctures from the article right through to the corkboard, but halfway down the hall she could see the article was missing.

She looked across the hall as if the culprit who had removed it might be hiding behind an open door. Stupid. Who would steal an article? Who would punch holes in one? She'd come for answers. Keesha's mother's door was still open and as she got closer, she could see Brenda Fletcher at her desk. Sara knocked on the doorjamb.

"Sara, come on in," she said as she stood up. "Are you looking for Keesha?" *Looking for Keesha?*

*No.* "I wanted to ask if I could have the article on me from the bulletin board when a new one goes up, but it's missing."

Brenda Fletcher's uncomfortable expression was the reply she'd been dreading. "It was damaged."

"Damaged?"

"Just this afternoon. I have no idea who did it and I'm terribly sorry."

"How was it damaged?"

"It was punctured."

# Chapter 18

Sara ached to tell Mrs. Fletcher what she knew. Brenda Fletcher was like a second mother. But she also knew school policy. Anything hinting of lousy citizenship would be mentioned in morning announcements or brought up at the next student assembly. Hardly what she had in mind for flushing out a stalker. And always, there were the social workers to think about. No matter how the school might handle it internally, they would be obligated to tell Youth Services.

She stayed quiet and accepted Mrs. Fletcher's apology for the "mean-spirited" prank.

"Any chance that you still have the article? Could I have it anyway?"

Mrs. Fletcher pulled it from her drawer. "I've already discussed it with Mr. Morrow. I guess you might as well take it." Then she invited Sara to dinner. This was one night Sara didn't want to eat alone.

"I'm so terribly sorry," Mrs. Fletcher reiterated as she walked with Sara to the door. "Coming right on the heels of that awful business with your dress at the cleaners must be unnerving."

"Did Keesha tell you?"

"No. Lucille Parnell mentioned that it turned out to be some disgruntled customer."

Sara frowned as she tried to read her lips.

Mrs. Fletcher bent her fingers in front of her face: *"angry customer."*

Sara nodded as she finally understood. "Yes, someone angry at the store. Steve found out." The lie made her face hot.

"You know Lucille. She'll probably be up with another casserole or something to cheer you up. She told me this afternoon how she worries about you and Steve."

"This afternoon?" *Afternoon?*

"Yes. She's down the hall telling the World Affairs Club about the latest prison reforms."

"Here?"

Mrs. Fletcher nodded. "She arrived about three."

In plenty of time to sabotage Kim's article and the one on the bulletin board. Sara's heart sank. Once again Suspect One had been joined by Suspect Two. Who'd suspect a busybody arriving with a casserole? The perfect alibi. Feed the poor parentless orphans on the seventh floor while she terrorized one of them. It probably made perfect sense to a stalker. Sara swallowed her bitterness. She led Tuck into the hall and waved good-bye to Keesha's mother till dinner. She couldn't wait for a home-cooked meal with the Fletchers.

The hall was deserted and most offices were closed for the day, but as she and Tuck headed for the back corridor, the door to the student lounge opened. Marcus Fletcher and half a dozen other members of the World Affairs Committee streamed out with hand-made posters. Mrs. Parnell was right behind him, deep in conversation. Before Sara could yank Tuck back, the woman stumbled against his tail and let out what Sara knew was a shriek. She stumbled back into Marcus.

"Filthy —" She flushed scarlet. ". . . scared the living daylights . . . in the building . . . animals."

Marcus was doing his best to calm her down as Sara apologized. It only added to the frenzy. Mrs. Parnell was frightened and embarrassed. Sara did her best to make amends, but the woman clearly wanted nothing but a quick exit. Sara obliged. Let Marcus explain that aid-dogs were allowed in public buildings. She hoped he added that this was her school, not the Thurston Court busybody's.

Sara wanted out of the building, out of the constantly creepy feeling that kept her on edge. She moved through the school with the urgency of a fire drill, as if she were heading for the safe exit. There was no safe exit. Even as she hustled past lockers and closed classrooms, she knew it would be worse once she was outside. It wasn't until she glanced at Tuck and realized he was trotting that she was aware of how fast she was moving. As if she could outrun it. It. Her. Him. She stopped and leaned back against the cool metal and pressed her arm across her forehead. Her ragged laugh caught in her throat.

Maybe Mike Lenza and Mrs. Parnell were in this together. Maybe they had some perverse connection to each other she hadn't figured out. She pounded her fist on the locker. That, of course, was what she needed: the connection, the clue, the thread that wove this nightmare together, the why behind all of it.

Tuck panted as he looked up at her. She moved painfully as she forced herself to slow down. Where stalkers were involved, there wasn't a why that made sense. Mike Lenza had no qualms about showing up at her locker. There wasn't a more obvious presence in the building than Mrs. Parnell's. She shivered as she tried to throw off the gooseflesh that made her skin crawl and wished she hadn't driven to school so that she could go home with Brenda Fletcher.

The shortest path to her car was through the gym. She reined Tuck's leash in as short as possible. The girls had finished their practice. Most were heading for the locker room while a few waved to her or talked to the coach. As Sara crossed from the hall entrance to the street exit, the boys who'd been waiting for their turn stomped down from the bleachers or began to run through drills under the baskets. The vibrations from the activity reverberated in her legs. Like the girls, a few nodded, waved, glanced at Tuck. She flushed as she stared back. Is it you? she wanted to scream. Or you? Or you?

The boys' coach put a metal whistle in his mouth. She tried to remember the sound as his team gathered. It would have been easy to give into the isolation that deafness forced on her. She'd fought that isolation daily since leaving Edgewood. Now she faced something worse, the isolation imposed by fear. She tugged Tuck's leash.

The parking lot was draped in dusky light. It would be dark by the time she got home, dark and silent and empty. As the heavy fire doors closed behind her, she spotted a teacher getting into his car. One of the janitors brought the day's trash to the Dumpster. The floodlights snapped on at the edge of the roof. There was no sign of Mike Lenza. Whether his goal had been the crew errand he'd mentioned or tormenting her with the articles, there was no sign of him or his car.

She wondered which car was Mrs.

Parnell's. Maybe she'd walked the few blocks from Thurston Court. Maybe she'd fly home on a broom. Maybe she'd get a ride home with Brenda Fletcher. Gruesome thought. Sara pulled her car keys from her pocket.

She went directly to Keesha's and checked in with Steve from there. He was due home by 9:30. Her troubling news would have to wait till then. Dinner at the Fletchers' was exactly what Sara needed. Marcus and Keesha had concocted their own lasagna recipe which their father John embellished with a tossed salad. Brenda Fletcher had picked up French bread and apple pie from a local bakery on her way home. It could have been a bowl of cereal for all Sara cared. She was hungry for the comradery, starving for the feeling of safety.

Keesha's mother apologized again for the vandalism of the newspaper article. Keesha put down her fork and signed to Sara. *You didn't tell me.*

*It just happened this afternoon.*

*"With that mess with your dress, weren't you scared?"*

Brenda Fletcher looked alarmed as she patted Sara's arm. "Keesha, there's no need to frighten Sara."

No, Sara wanted to reply. Someone else is doing a damn good job already.

As promised, Steve came home on time and joined Sara in their den. He put his hand on her shoulder. "Better day?"

Sara tried to smile, but emotion shredded her composure. Angrily she yanked the box from the bookshelf and showed him Kim's article and the one from the bulletin board. His handsome features darkened as his mouth tightened to a thin, grim line. "What the hell!"

*There were two. This one was posted on the bulletin board.* "Pinned up at school in the hall outside the business office. Right in the administrative wing." Her anger rose in waves as she thought about how brazen someone would have to be. "Whoever did it took big chances. Kim's was by the gym.

Lots of students. Easy. But the other one was right in the hall with Mr. Morrow's office — Head of School — everybody in charge is in that hall."

Spots of color dotted his cheeks. "It's a game, Sara. Someone is trying to see how close he or she can get to you without being caught. A psychologist would probably say it was no accident that whoever this is picked something as obvious as the bulletin board."

"Obvious?" She tapped her temple. Had she understood? "Not obvious. Sneaky. Hiding all the time."

Steve shook his head. "Whoever is doing this isn't hiding. The perp is right out in the open." *You must feel it. Two steps in front of you or two steps behind.* He hugged her, but she pushed him away.

*Catch him! Catch her! Whoever it is will slip up sooner or later. They always do. Isn't that what Dad always said?*

Steve frowned and she could tell he was at a loss to understand her.

"Dad used to say there's always a slip or a clue that's been right under your nose all the time," she said as clearly as possible.

Steve sighed and shoved his hand through his hair. "Lieutenant Marino was there today. She stopped by to line things up."

Sara arched her eyebrow. *Never saw her.* "Did she say she saw Mike Lenza or Mrs. Parnell?"

Steve shook his head. He looked exhausted as he walked to the window. Sara waited while he stared unfocused on the skyline. When he turned back to her, the color had left his complexion. "She saw Bret Sanderson."

*Not Bret, M-I-K-E!*

Steve shook his head. "Bret was at school. You'd already left with Kim."

It must have been someone else. Sara pointed angrily to her TTY. *He would have called. There would be a message.* She shoved the words at him with angry gestures and scowls, but as Steve slowly shook his head, she sank back against the chair. She didn't need her brother to remind her that Rosemary Marino wouldn't have made a mistake. The officer knew Bret. They'd been in this apartment together. They'd been at functions together on other cases. There was no mistaking the tall basketball player. *Not Bret.*

"Bret was in the building this afternoon."

"Not doing anything."

Again Steve moved with reluctance. He put his hand in his pocket and the other on her shoulder. "When Rosemary spotted him, he was in the back corridor by the gym. He waited for a few minutes, then swore and dropped something. He left through the parking lot." Slowly he withdrew his hand from his pocket and opened it in front of her. In it was a paper clip with one end bent open.

# Chapter 19

"This is how people get framed," she cried. Was she screaming? The words blazed in her head as she formed them, spit them at her brother. *It isn't Bret. It can't be Bret!*

Steve grabbed her by the shoulders. "Do you think I want it to be Bret! He's been great for you. Supportive." He tapped his chin angrily for her to pay attention. "I had no reason to suspect him except for all this coincidental stuff."

*Say again.*

*He's been in the wrong place at the right time. Many times.* "That's the way these things work. That's the way these people operate. Don't keep anything from me, Sara. Someone who thinks he loves you can get it all confused, all turned around inside. You could wind up —" He shut his eyes. "Never mind. Never mind. Just don't fight me on this. I'm a cop. I see this stuff every day."

She gasped and shook off his grasp. *Dead!* "You were going to say the stalker wants me dead."

Steve's glance turned icy, professional. "The stalker wants you to pay attention. That can mean anything to someone who isn't thinking straight. God knows, I don't want it to be Bret, but for now he's put himself on the list. If I weren't chaperoning the dance next week, I'd have you break the date. No game tomorrow night."

"But I'm going with Keesha and Liz and Kim. You said you'd go."

"That was before this latest —"

"Send Lieutenant Marino with us. An undercover cop should do the trick."

"I know you're angry —"

She tried to catch her breath. *Sorry, Bret. I can't sit in the bleachers and watch you play tomorrow night because I think you sliced my dress and left weird messages on my brother's answering machine, and punched a million holes in the newspaper article* — A sob caught in her throat.

Steve tapped his mouth. He didn't understand.

It was more than language. No one understood. She tapped her ear angrily. "How am I supposed to go to school? How am I supposed to stay in the empty apartment while you're at work? How am I supposed to get a normal life when I can't trust anybody?"

The tears sprang from her lower lids. "All I want is what everybody else has. Normal days. Normal nights. Normal friends." In quick succession she signed words she knew Steve recognized, not caring if they put more pain in his expression. *Deaf. Orphan. Cop. Stalker.*

"Sara, stop!"

*Then tell me when I get to be normal.*

The next night Sara jumped to her feet with the rest of the Penham School fans who filled the bleachers. She thought of Mr. Hagstrom and his biology principles. Osmosis. If she stood there with everybody else, the excitement was bound to rub off, to sink in, to seep right into her cells. If she could just get into the spirit of the game, there wouldn't be room for the dread.

As their star senior sank a basket from midcourt, the Boosters Club began to clap. To her right, Keesha, Liz, and Kim followed the rhythm directed by the cheerleaders while Bret hustled back into formation with his team. She tried to make eye contact with him, but he was looking at his coach.

On her left Steve was whistling through his teeth. Marisa Douglas was laughing at him. She had to hand it to Marisa. Going to a Friday night high school basketball game could hardly be her idea of a romantic evening. This time next week she'd have to chaperon the Harvest Dance with him. That was enough teenage activity.

What reason had Steve given Marisa for accompanying his younger sister to her boyfriend's basketball game? Boyfriend. Bret hadn't called. She'd ached to ask him why he'd been at school and not told her, but she hadn't heard a word from him. Before the game he'd been surrounded by players. She wanted to sign to him now, right across the gymnasium. *Why didn't you call me last night?*

She'd gone to bed exhausted by the tension but too uneasy to sleep. It felt like hours that she'd stayed a coiled spring as she pounded the pillow, sure that any minute the TTY light would blink, or Steve would call her to the phone. She'd finally fallen into a restless sleep.

Maybe Steve was right: She shouldn't have come. She didn't feel safe. She didn't feel anything. For all she knew her brother had scattered half the Penn Street police force among the fans behind her. Sara had spotted Lieutenant Marino twice at school. She'd been sitting in the teachers' lounge midmorning as Sara passed the doorway on the way to biology. After lunch she'd spotted her handing out drug awareness pamphlets to the fifth-grade health class.

Friday had been a safe, uneventful day: no Mike, no Mrs. Parnell. No Bret. Maybe she had the lieutenant to thank; maybe not. Uneventful or not, it would be a long time until anything felt normal.

Penham beat Valley by six points, but the

close victory and hard effort didn't change Bret's demeanor. As they'd planned, she met him outside the locker rooms after he'd showered and changed. He suggested Mario's, a sports hangout close to the school. It didn't seem to bother him that Steve and Marisa drove, slid into the booth with them, and dropped him back at his own car in the school parking lot when they finished at the restaurant.

Steve had warned her ahead of time not to suggest that they take separate cars or that Bret drive her home. She didn't, but the shock was that Bret didn't suggest it either. Instead he kissed her once and slid from the backseat of the Howells' sedan, and signed *thanks.*

*Have fun with your grandparents,* she added.

*Sure thing.* He put his hand to his ear to indicate a phone.

Sara nodded. "I'll call you" had no more significance than "see you around." It had started to rain as they returned to school, a drizzle which matched her mood. In the front seat Marisa slid closer to Steve as he turned on the windshield wipers. In the back, Sara pressed her fists to her eyes, grateful for the dark. Her fear was fused with a major dose of heartache. It was a strangling combination.

*Come over and drag yourself through my closet,* Keesha signed Saturday as they finished lunch in Sara's empty apartment. Rain fell in sheets across the window, the perfect afternoon to oil her mountain bike and store it for the winter, but she was in no mood to hang around alone in the basement. Instead she'd dragged out lunch with Keesha till nearly two o'clock.

*I need something for the dance,* Keesha was saying. She paused. *Are you going to buy something new to replace the ruined dress?*

Sara shrugged.

*You okay?* "I know you've been bummed out all week about the dress —"

*Say again.*

Keesha brought her open fingers down from her face. *Sad. Angry about your dress.*

*I have another dress I can wear. If I go,* Sara signed.

*If you go. So that's it. You and Bret are on

*the outs. I thought so. You've been miserable, tense.* She raised and lowered her shoulders. *No fun at the game last night. Fight?*

*Sort of. I know we were all going to go out to dinner before the dance, but you and Jason should make your own plans. I don't want to foul anything up.*

Keesha paused. *Okay, if that's what you want. I thought you were upset about the newspaper article. Don't be. Somebody's just jealous that you're getting so much attention lately. You have tons of friends. Want to talk about Bret? Do you think he wants to date somebody else?*

No, my brother thinks he might be the one who slit my dress with a razor and has managed to terrorize me since last Sunday. Sara stuck the last part of her sandwich in her mouth. For once she was glad to follow Steve's advice. Keesha would think she was the crazy one if she told her anything. She chewed and swallowed.

She couldn't — wouldn't — believe that Bret was the stalker, but that did nothing to soothe the pain of the last twenty-four hours. *Things aren't right between us now. That's all I know. He and his family left this morning till Wednesday. Family stuff. I can't talk to him. I don't want to talk about him either. It just depresses me.*

She sipped her milk. She didn't want to talk about anything. She wanted to think. Bret aside, Keesha had just hit on a motive Sara hadn't considered. Jealousy. What had she done to the stalker that might have made him or her jealous? Who could be jealous of a deaf orphan?

## Chapter 20

Between the two of them, they came up with a sophisticated outfit for Keesha to wear, but it took most of the afternoon. She was going with Jason Woods, who was also taking her to a movie that night. Sara laughed at her best friend's halfhearted invitation that Sara go with them.

*First date. And me in the backseat? I don't think so. My only date tonight's with Tuck.*

She crossed the hall guiltily. She was overdue and Tuck would let her know it. John O'Connor walked the retriever for them whenever the Howells' schedule was too full, but this week Tuck had been spoiled. She let him run on the soccer field during lunch, patted him in class . . .

Steve didn't want her out alone, but it was pouring buckets. She wasn't about to ask Keesha to get drenched with her. Besides, even a stalker wouldn't go out in this weather.

She opened the apartment door carefully, afraid Tuck would be bounding through the foyer at the sound of the key. There was no sign of him. She slapped her thigh and walked down the narrow hall to her bedroom. He was still curled in his favorite spot at the foot of her bed. As she knelt with the leash he finally raised his head.

*Fine with me if we stay in, Tuck. It's just your kidneys I'm thinking of.* She ruffled his fur. While he stretched and finally shook himself out, Sara glanced across the hall. The laundry basket outside the bathroom door was full again. Steve could do it this time. Let the cop deal with the demons in the basement.

She walked Tuck to the foyer, grabbed an umbrella, and put on her foul weather slicker. Demons in the basement. Because of the stalker she had to drag her dog to school, put up with undercover cops following her every move, maybe screw up some of the best friendships she had. Sara yanked the wash into her arms and with the umbrella on top, rode the elevator to the basement.

Her stomach was in knots but the stalker was not going to make her afraid in her own apartment building. She gathered her courage as she had gathered the dirty clothes. Maybe she'd work on her bike after all.

The basement hall was still dimly lit and smelled of disinfectant and fabric softener. The light had been repaired, however, and Mrs. Parnell wasn't sitting in the corner, eyeing Sara over her novel. Where was the relief? Sara loaded the machine and got it running, then nudged Tuck in the direction of the stairwell for the climb to the lobby, one flight up.

Thurston Court had ten floors of living space. Sara opened the heavy fire door and looked up inside the gray tower of steel stairs. If she leaned over the railing, she could see the red glow of the exit sign over some of the doors on the floors above. She felt the vibrations of a slamming door and craned her neck. Somewhere above her someone had gone back into the hall or come into the stairwell. Her deafness made it impossible to judge distance. Tuck refused to climb.

*Only one flight, silly, not all ten.*

He sat at her feet, attentive enough to frighten her.

Slowly she looked back up the stairs and unconsciously moved back against the wall while she caught her breath. She counted four railings. Above her, at the fourth railing, a shadow moved against the wall. It stopped. How much sound did her breathing make? She pressed her hand to her mouth and then to her heart. One flight in the elevator was the height of laziness but Tuck didn't want the stairs anymore than she did.

She turned around. The small pane of glass in the middle of the basement door was blocked from the outside by what looked like cardboard. She pushed the bar to open it. It gave less than an inch. Someone had deliberately shut her in.

Before panic could steal what was left of her common sense, she threw her weight against the door, then again. It wouldn't budge.

Tuck stood alert then took his cue from her. He pawed at the jamb as if he could dig their way out. She ached to hear the growl she knew was coming from his throat. She looked over her shoulder, up into the cavernous stairwell then shoved again against the door. This time it gave and she half tumbled into the hall as a red-faced delivery man kept her from falling.

There were two of them, flushed and surprised. Between them a six-foot container was strapped on a dolly. REFRIGERATOR\THIS END UP was stamped just below the line of the glass pane in the fire door.

The flush spread up from collars to their eyebrows. "What, are you deaf?" one of them said.

The other added, "I said, 'Just a minute.' The damn thing slipped off the dolly, all right? What's your hurry?"

*I am deaf. I didn't hear. I didn't know.* She circled her heart not caring that they were confused and embarrassed. She yanked Tuck past the open service elevator and took him out through the garage.

You can't make me scared of my own shadow. She tapped out the internal message to the rhythm of Tuck's reluctant trot. *You can't.* She huddled deeper into her slicker as they walked, and repeated her directive. Dad would be so angry. He'd worked so hard to make sure her world stayed wide open. The Edgewood School for the Deaf had taught her to communicate and insured her place in the deaf community, but he'd also balanced it with the hearing world. Keesha's ASL lessons and the Howells' were each part of insuring her independence. Now some half-crazed stalker was ruining everything. She was terror-struck by her own imagination.

She crossed the street as obvious as a school bus in her yellow rain gear. Her heart had calmed down, but the adrenaline continued to pump, driven by anger. Someone might get her in a dingy basement, or an empty stairwell, but she was dealing with a coward. She hadn't been approached or challenged or even frightened in public. Every threat, every bizarre object had been planted in her absence. This wimp worked when she was away from him. From her. As meager as they were, she needed to list her clues as much as she needed to collect the evidence.

That night Sara told Steve about the stairwell and the refrigerator incident as well as her theory.

"You may be absolutely right," he said as he sipped his coffee, "but that doesn't mean I want you anywhere by yourself." He tapped his chest. *Me, Tuck, Keesha. I want you to see your other friends only at our place or at the Fletchers', nowhere else, until we have a better idea —*

She put her hands over his to stop him. "This creep is putting me in prison."

"That might be part of the plan . . . to box you in, make you afraid to go anywhere. Whoever it is will trip up, they always do. I'm sorry we have to include Bret."

Sara shrugged but it wasn't enough to dissolve the stab of pain. "You might have to chaperon the dance for nothing."

"Don't break the date unless you'll go without him. This is one time I do want you with Bret. I have to be at the dance and I'd rather have you there where I can see you and keep an eye on him than have you home."

"In case he knows I'm home and hides out in the laundry room? I can't believe I said that."

Steve shrugged. "Even Marisa noticed how strained things were between you two last night."

She missed it. *Say again.*

*Things were not good last night.*

Sara hated to agree. *Weird. Strange.* "He's not himself. Maybe he wants to break up." She put her hand out to silence her brother. *I know, I know. He hates me or secretly is jealous of me so instead of breaking up, he's just going to stalk me to death.*

*No joke,* Steve signed back angrily.

Sara looked into his troubled expression. "I can't remember the last time I thought anything was funny."

## Chapter 21

I can't do this. I can't sit here and eat waffles with Keesha and Marcus as if nothing's wrong. She gave Steve what passed for an enthusiastic smile. That was the best she could do. His idea of having Sunday brunch with friends as close as these was torture. They knew her too well. They'd been through too much with her already not to know that life at the Howells' was not running smoothly.

As soon as they'd finished, she used the excuse to flee to her room. Let Steve invent something if they asked.

The rain had stopped, but it had knocked off the last of the leaves from the trees. The November sky was still the color of steel. Are you happy? She looked down at the street. I'm running away from my own friends, not just you. *Whoever you are. Wherever you are,* she jabbed out as she turned from the window.

At two o'clock Steve left for "parts unknown" as Sara called his undercover assignment. He was dressed for the docks again, for blending in with people he didn't like her to think about. Normally she had to work at not thinking about what he might be facing, but that was before she'd become obsessed with her own situation. Normal. There it was again.

"Make another stab at your English paper this afternoon," Steve said as he hugged her good-bye.

She pantomimed a dagger. *I can't spend the whole day in my room. It feels like prison.*

Ten minutes later she was staring into the box of evidence. Stab. Some detectives they were. She pulled out both copies of the article and held them up to the lamp. A hodgepodge of tiny points of light shone back to her. No pattern, no message spelled out, just holes. She tried to count and gave up at seventy. It could have been done in less than a minute. Bing, bing, bing, bing, bing. Stab and run. She gritted her teeth. Stab and run, Steve, not stab and stand in the gym corridor bending the paper clip.

She put down the newsprint and took a paper clip off the desk, then bent it open. Her hand shook but she managed to slip the sharp metal prong cleanly through the first hole. A perfect match. She tried another, then another. Pain radiated behind her ribs. It's not Bret. It can't be Bret. She squinted at the paper, into hole after hole, until she was cross-eyed. Traces of something were evident on more than half, minuscule lines on one edge, then another. Graphite. Pencil points, not paper clips. It could be. She rifled the desk for a magnifying glass but couldn't recall that they'd ever had one.

Proof. The Sunday paper lay unread in the living room. She tried to rouse Tuck to go with her, but he lay on his side, dead to the world. Instead she darted from the apartment and down the hall to the incinerator room and grabbed a used newspaper from the stack to be recycled.

When she got back to the apartment, she pinned a piece of newsprint to her bulletin board and stabbed it with a sharpened pencil from the cup on her desk. Angry stabs, as full of hate as she could muster, then hurried stabs, as if Mrs. Fletcher or Mr. Morrow would appear in the hall at any minute. She bent another paper clip and eased it into the pencil holes. Over and over, it was a perfect match.

The final proof sat on the shelf in the back of her closet. Next to a stack of textbooks she'd brought with her from Edgewood was a science kit from her childhood. She'd loved it. Her father had called her his junior forensics expert. She set the microscope up on the desk and slid the real article under it. It took less than a heartbeat to focus the lens. Graphite lined the holes. It was unmistakable: The stalker had used a pencil, not a paper clip.

The euphoria lasted until she scooped out Tuck's dinner. All right, she was no closer to the perp. It proved that it wasn't Bret Sanderson. She didn't care that Bret was about as likely a suspect as Keesha. Her batteries were recharged. It gave her something to show

Steve; it gave her control. She wrinkled her nose at the aroma of canned dog food and knocked the remains into the dish of kibble, then picked up the water dish to freshen it.

She paused. There were traces of crimson drifting on the surface of the water. Some had settled on the bottom. She carried Tuck's dish to the sink and snapped on the bright overhead light. Even in the gray winter's light across the kitchen she could tell it was blood.

Tuck was still asleep in the den. He'd been asleep or lethargic all day, for a few days if she stopped and thought about it. She'd had to drag him around the basement yesterday; he wouldn't climb the stairs. She'd been giving him a lot of exercise. It could just be overexertion.

Sara ruffled his fur as she knelt next to him in the living room, but dread began its slow seep into her bones. The leash in the laundry, barking on the answering machine, Tuck's missing photo — all were dog related. Since Tuesday threats against Tuck had been escalating. Mrs. Parnell hates dogs. Mike Lenza could, too, for all she knew.

*Was the stalker in the stairwell yesterday or were you sick, Tuck? Did Steve run you too hard this morning? Did he run you at all?* She hadn't thought to ask. Exhaustion didn't explain the blood in the water. Gently she eased his mouth open. Traces of blood rimmed his teeth on the right side. She tried to make him sit up so she could see the other side. Tuck's worst habit was sniffing anything and everything in his path. Glass, she thought as she gingerly pressed her finger above the blood. It would be just like him to have crunched down on something sharp and cut his gums or tongue. Anything sharp could have been swallowed, as well. Worry heated her nerves. *Do you hurt, Tuck?*

She pressed her ear to his side as if she could hear something. Angrily, she knocked her ear. She couldn't tell whether he was in pain or not, but he was obviously in no mood to go anywhere, including the kitchen for dinner.

Sara left him on the rug. Steve was unreachable. She wished she'd gone with the Fletchers. She went back to Tuck with a paper towel and patted his mouth. He didn't wince or snarl. She supposed that meant no pain which probably meant no cut. Bleeding gums. Maybe it was some dental problem, but bad teeth wouldn't make him sleep so much.

She opened the cabinet door in the kitchen next to the phone where her father had always kept emergency and commonly used phone numbers. Gina Agnew, DVM was listed next to their family doctor. She memorized the number and went to her TTY to use the relay operator. An appointment for Sunday evening was a long shot, but she gave the answering service all the pertinent information she could think of. Ten minutes later the vet returned the call through the operator. **Bring Tuck right in. I'll be waiting** was typed out on her display board.

Gina Agnew's office was near the Radley University campus where she taught in the veterinary medical school. It was the same residential neighborhood as the Sandersons'. Sara gave his street one quick glance. Bret would have come. He would have helped get Tuck into the car, the old Bret, anyway.

Tuck was cooperative. He got himself out of the car, albeit without the usual frantic tail waving and excitement that usually ensued with his infrequent visits. Sara offered up a silent prayer as she opened the office door. Not Tuck. Don't take Tuck.

The office smelled as it always did of disinfectant and animals, dogs primarily. No wonder Tuck loved the foyer. She was the only client, Tuck the only new patient. Within moments Sara was standing across the stainless-steel examining table from Dr. Agnew. For long, painful minutes she'd kept her hand on Tuck's side while the doctor examined the traces of blood on his teeth, listened to his heart, looked at his eyes and ears, felt his internal organs. Every probe brought a frown or a nod. The wait was torture.

Dr. Agnew took the stethoscope from her ears and looked at Sara. "I'm sorry."

Sara put her hands out as if she were warding off a punch. "No."

## Chapter 22

Dr. Agnew raised her own hand. "It's serious, very serious, but not necessarily fatal. I'll have him moved to the University Animal Hospital. He's all right . . . so far. I won't have any answers until we run blood, stool, urine tests, maybe even liver function. You were right to bring him in. The bleeding gums are a sign of poisoning, but his pulse and heart are strong. I doubt he ate enough to kill him."

"Ate. On purpose?"

"Hard to say. Dogs get into things, even on leashes. Do you have reason to think he was poisoned on purpose?"

Sara tapped her ear.

"Does someone want to poison him?" Dr. Agnew repeated.

Sara's nod was slow and reluctant. "We had a threat."

The vet arched her eyebrows. "I've seen plenty of cases of household rat poison, mouse repellent wrapped up in some meat, left out where a dog or cat will get it. It doesn't show up for the first few days."

"Do you think he ate it Thursday or Friday?"

"Possibly." She tapped her own gums. "It shows up here. I'll keep him here under observation while we do the tests."

The irony was obvious. All week she'd changed her routine for her own safety. All week he'd been on different routes, even with Steve. She shuddered. All week Tuck had also been at school. She walked him every lunch period in the same place at the edge of the soccer field. How many times had she let him run without his leash? He was safe inside the fenced-in school property, she wanted to add. Safe from cars, traffic . . .

No tears. Not one more damn tear would

fall because of the creep that was doing this. Not one. Instead Sara straightened up. "I'll tell Steve. He'll want to call you." She pantomimed the phone.

Dr. Agnew nodded and touched her arm. "If there's no organ damage — liver or kidneys — Tuck should recover."

Once she was back in her car, Sara gripped the steering wheel and pressed her head against it. No tears. No tears. Traffic was light. There was still enough moisture in the air that she had to run the windshield wipers.

She looked at the headlights in the rearview mirror, unable to judge whether she was being followed. This time as she came to the intersection where Bret's street intersected, she turned right. The car behind her did, too. She'd only meant to cruise past the Sandersons', but as the headlights advanced in her rearview mirror, she pulled sharply into Bret's driveway. She strained to see if Mike Lenza were in the driver's seat, but it was dark, and wet, and she knew her imagination was running wild. The car coasted past until it was just a blur of red taillights as it continued into the darkness.

She stayed in the driveway long enough to collect her thoughts. *You would have helped, Bret.* She looked up at the dark windows before pulling away from the curb and heading for Thurston Court. Thirty minutes later she was back at Thurston Court. The apartment hadn't felt this empty since she was six years old.

*. . . Tuck should recover.* Sara finished signing the night's events to Steve at 11 P.M. She kept her lower lip firmly between her teeth. True to her word she didn't cry. She used anger, more anger than she knew she possessed, to keep herself focused. "Tuck's out of the way." She held up her fingers and ticked off the clues. "First barking on the tape machine. Leash in the dryer, then the picture gone from my locker. Maybe the stalker was after Tuck."

Steve didn't reply, instead he tapped his temple, indicating for Sara to pay attention. "You are not to play detective. I don't want you anywhere near the soccer field where you walked Tuck. Don't go thinking you can come up with whatever poisoned him." He made an *X* over his heart. *Promise.*

"There might be evidence sitting out there."

*Promise! We'll take care of it.*

They exchanged glances. She knew from his expression that he was thinking what she was. The stalker's goal might have been to get rid of Tuck. Or it might — just as easily — have been to get rid of Tuck in order to get to her. She'd have her answer soon enough.

Monday was a normal day, if she dared to use the word. There was no sign of Mike Lenza. Mrs. Parnell might have been at her apartment window with binoculars, but she never saw her. Without Tuck to walk, Sara went directly to school and came home after her workout session with the crew team. Everyone missed Tuck. She said his visits had been only an experiment.

At lunch she'd spotted Lieutenant Marino at the edge of the soccer field. She looked like she was getting in some noontime exercise between drug awareness classes, but Sara knew better. *Search*, she said to herself. *Comb the area for a scrap of meat, something that might look like bait.*

The few students and faculty who commented on Tuck's absence were given the same explanation. She told them all that she didn't need him. Tuck was at home, as always. Every time she said it her scalp tingled. *Somebody knows I'm lying*, she thought more than once as she walked the halls. *And I'll find you before you find me.*

Tuesday was as uneventful as Monday. Tuck's condition was listed as stable. Steve was adamant that the stalker would be waiting for Sara to visit, but finally agreed to take her in an unmarked police car with scanner and two-way radio. The pedigreed golden retriever was hardly himself, but he wasn't the limp rag she'd brought to Dr. Agnew, either. He wagged his tail slowly as she and her brother knelt to pat him. It was Steve who had tears in his eyes.

*I'm so sorry*, Sara signed to Tuck. *Some-*

*body's sicker than you, sick and mean and dangerous.*

Sara made it through Wednesday's classes, and left through the gym entrance where Steve had insisted on picking her up. As she closed the car door after her, she caught sight of a blue sports car leaving the parking lot. It was partially blocked by a school bus.

She turned to Steve as he tapped her arm. "Sara, what is it?"

"Nothing."

He stopped the car so they could face each other. "Don't tell me nothing. I can read your face. What did you see?"

She pointed to the now-empty space. "I saw a car that might have been Mike Lenza's leaving the parking lot. Over there." Steve craned his neck to see around the bus. "Can you be sure?"

"No. That's why I didn't say anything. No problems today, either. Good day, in fact."

"Mike would recognize this car." Her brother put the car in park and took his foot off the brake. "Rosemary hasn't come up with anything. Whoever it is has backed off. I heard from the vet, too." *Dog doctor called. Some of the tests are back.*

*Poison?* "Poison?"

Steve nodded. "They're guessing common stuff for rats and mice. More tests back tomorrow."

On Thursday Bret was home. Sara had no idea what time he'd gotten in the night before, but there had been no phone call. Steve drove her to school on his way to the county courthouse downtown. He was scheduled to spend the day in court and he looked ready for business in a sports blazer, tie, and dark-gray slacks. It was a far cry from the undercover garb he usually wore. A day in court meant he'd be home for dinner. Although he wouldn't discuss the case, chances were good that it was drug or theft related. For the first time since his tires had been slashed, she was worried about Steve instead of herself. It almost felt odd to have nothing upsetting her own routine, but it was impossible to tell if the change was permanent, or part of the psychological terror she'd been wrapped in for a week and a half. She counted backward on her fingers. The trip to the vet marked a week of the torment. This was day twelve.

There was no crew practice and she hated to turn down Kim's invitation to go with Liz, Keesha, and her to check out decorations for the dance. I have promises to keep: no friends except on my own territory. She waved them off and walked toward home. Broad daylight, change of routine. This time no sign of Mike Lenza's car. She was following Steve's directions and added half an hour to her trip by stopping at the Penn Street Deli for some of the Patrones' barbecued chicken. A late afternoon sun poked through the clouds as she left the shop. Today the neighborhood smelled like vanilla cookies.

The doorman was on his rounds. She checked the mail. No flower pasted on the buzzer; no rose in the bushes, nothing. It didn't ease the stress of opening the empty apartment once she got upstairs.

She dropped her backpack in the den. The answering machine light was blinking, but she kept her uneasiness down to a weak case of chills. She stared at the machine, then dismissed it. The vet was due to call; Marisa; one of Steve's friends; something normal, mundane. . . . Steve would be home in a while. He could listen.

She changed into jeans and a cotton turtleneck, then shoved the sleeves up to her elbows. It was about time she and her brother had a decent meal. She decided on green beans and mashed potatoes. When she set the oven to keep the chicken warm, she opened the refrigerator. A bakery box was on the shelf under the milk, like the one Mrs. Fletcher had brought home the night Sara had eaten with them.

The Fletchers had a key to the apartment and it would be just like one of them to slip a pie into the fridge. Of course it could always be another disgusting mushroom concoction from Mrs. Parnell. She fumbled with the string knot then gave up and grabbed a paring knife to cut it. Lemon meringue, she hoped. It had been their favorite since childhood. Sara flipped the top back and peered in.

She gasped as her heart threw itself against her ribs. She dropped the box upright and backed away with such force, she knocked the vase of Bret's flowers over. Water ran across the kitchen table and onto the floor. It wasn't a pie, it was cake, frosted with white icing. In the middle was the picture of Tuck.

The photo from her locker had been trimmed neatly around his shape. It was impaled in the frosting with pins at each corner, four of them sticking out in odd directions. "You're Next" was written on the cake in fancy, professional letters.

## Chapter 23

Sara gripped the knife and looked across the kitchen to the foyer. Someone had gotten into the apartment. She ached for Tuck. He alerted her to every noise, every shadow. He would have gone into the living room for her, or down the hall to the bedrooms. He'd nudge her, paws on her legs to tell her she wasn't alone. She wiped her sweaty hands on her jeans. That was the point, of course. To get rid of Tuck.

Get out. Get out, she said to herself. Before she realized what she'd done, she was out in the hall, the key in her pocket, the door shut. She ran with the box, trying to rid herself of the terrifying feeling that she was being followed. Fear propelled her down the hall to the elevator. Her apartment door stayed shut. No one had come out after her.

She stopped at the incinerator room and tried to catch her breath. This aberration belonged with the trash, the garbage. . . . Her head began to clear. This was evidence. The crime lab could do tests. If this cake was poisoned they could match the poison to Tuck's. There might be fingerprints on the photo. Steve would be home soon. Mike Lenza might be lurking somewhere waiting for her reaction, or Mrs. Parnell's twisted brain might have figured she'd run downstairs to stay with her, right into the spider's web. She'd wait with the doorman. It was the safest thing she could think of.

She couldn't go back into the apartment, so she put the cake box down in the corner of the incinerator room, next to the pile of newspapers waiting for recycling. She immediately recognized the sports page on the top of the pile. A scream she couldn't hear ripped from her throat.

DEAF ROWER TRIUMPHS had been neatly altered. This time, no puncture marks, no tears in the paper. The *F* had been changed to a *D* with a black pen. TRIUMPHS had been cleanly razor-bladed out and replaced with blank newsprint. The headline now read: DEAD ROWER. Under it Sara Howell still smiled with her teammates.

He's here. She's here. Sara choked as she held back sobs and gave in to her terror. She huddled on the floor with the cake and the newspaper. She stared at the open door. Out in the hall someone could be searching, or calling . . . or stalking. She couldn't hear, wouldn't know.

She stood up and tried to calm her ragged breathing. Mike Lenza couldn't get into the apartment. He wouldn't know about the incinerator room. It had to be someone familiar with the building. Someone who'd already been to the Howells' with a casserole, food for the grieving orphans. Someone who hated dogs.

She needed the elevator. She'd get downstairs to John and wait for Steve. She moved cautiously into the hall in time to see a figure. Bret Sanderson was walking down the corridor toward her, halfway between her apartment and the elevator.

Their eyes locked and he began to run. The basketball star took long, easy strides. He'd be beside her in a flash. Sara bolted ahead of him, but the only escape was the fire exit, the steel staircase at the far end of the hall. Not Bret! She'd proved it hadn't been Bret, even if he wanted to break up. . . .

Air burned in her lungs as she reached the door and yanked it open. She tumbled into the stairwell and looked down the eight flights to the basement. The stairs Tuck wouldn't climb, the stairs she'd been so sure had held the stalker on Saturday. She barely got to her feet when the door flew open again. Bret reached her, as she scrambled down the first flight. She felt his hand graze her shoulder. He grabbed and missed. She leaned, tumbled, tore down another flight, but his stride was twice the length of hers. He met her as she reached the landing of the sixth floor and pulled her into a hug, but this one was ironclad. When she threw her head back to free herself, he clamped his free hand over her mouth.

His handsome features had begun to transform. "Quiet," he demanded.

Sara tried to read his dark eyes as she fought, but the harder she struggled, the fiercer his grasp.

"Sara! Stop. It's all right. It's only me. What on earth —" He shoved her firmly down to the top step and opened his hands in a stop motion as he began to sign. *What scared you? Who did you think I was? Are you all right? What* — He sank down next to her and picked up the paring knife. *Sara, what the hell is this? What's going on?*

It wasn't until she caught her breath that she realized how pale he was. The color returned in splotches across his cheekbones. He was as frightened as she was.

*You're stalking me. You've been doing terrible things since I got back from the regatta. . . .*

*Me? What things? What's happened?*

*You know!* She thrust her fingers angrily at his eyes.

*All I know is that you've been acting strange, avoiding me, hanging around with a new guy and making me miserable.*

*Miserable. Say again?*

*That kid you met rowing.* He finger spelled
*M-I-K-E L-E —*

*I'm not hanging around with him! I'm
scared of him. I thought he was the one doing
this, until now, until you put the cake in my
refrigerator, until you hid in the apartment
just now. Until —*

She couldn't get the words out fast
enough. They tumbled from her hands as
they would have tumbled from her throat.
She should be more frightened. She should
flee, but the fear had been dissolved by her
breaking heart. *How could you poison Tuck?*

*What? Sara! I haven't been in your apart-
ment. The doorman let me up because he
knew you were in.* He tapped her forehead.
*You would have seen the blinking light for the
doorbell. I was running down the hall because I heard you scream in that storage
room. Sara, I have no idea what you're talking about. Poison Tuck? Me!*

*Thursday. You were at school last Thurs-
day without telling me.*

*Without telling you! I drove over to see if
you wanted to come watch me in a scrim-*

*mage, then afterward we could talk things out. Someone said you'd already left with M-I-K-E. It was the last straw. You've been so strange around me I had to find out what was going on. I finally found out it was somebody new. I figured he was the guy who sent you the rose, your secret admirer or something, he's the guy you thought you were talking to that time on your TTY.*

*Friday night after the game I waited for you to bring him up, to at least admit that you liked this guy. You didn't. I left for my grand-parents'. I was miserable the whole time I was out there. I want things cleared up once and for all.* He tapped her shoulder and his. *You and me, Sara. Forget our date for tomor-row night. You can take M-I-K-E to the dance. I don't care anymore, but what's the screaming? Why did you think I was chasing you?*

Sara shook her head and pulled the mass of long brown hair back from her eyes. She started to laugh with relief, but tears filled her eyes, anyway. She walked with Bret back up to the seventh floor. By the time they'd been to the incinerator room and taken the elevator down to the doorman, she'd explained everything that had happened in the long, painful days since the rose had been taped to the door.

John O'Connor had just finished signing for a package as they got off the elevator. Sara spoke as clearly as she could. "Did Mrs. Parnell give you a bakery box to leave in our refrigerator this afternoon?"

He shook his head. "The box was on my desk when I got back from lunch. Typed note said Howell Seven-C." He leaned over and fished it from the trash basket. "I assumed you'd had it ordered and I missed the delivery guy."

"Have you seen Mrs. Parnell lately?"

The doorman shook his head. "She's out of town. She's been gone since the weekend with her theater club in New York. I'm holding her mail and newspapers."

They all turned their heads as a squad car pulled up to the front door. Steve Howell got out of the passenger seat. The minute he grinned, Sara knew there'd been trouble. He was no better at faking composure than she was.

# Chapter 24

Steve admitted that the unmarked police car he'd driven to the courthouse had had a tire slashed, one he'd changed himself, and that the department had insisted on impounding the car to go over it completely. The minute Sara told him of the trouble at Thurston Court his focus changed. He asked Bret to stay.

They ate the dinner Sara had been in the midst of preparing. While Steve brought the cake and newspaper from the incinerator room, Sara mopped up the flowers that still lay spilled over the kitchen table. After they ate, Steve went over the entire collection of evidence with Bret and this time asked for help.

Steve tried to sign, but as always it came out a jumble of what he knew and what he made up. He pointed first to Bret, then to his sister. *"You and you. At the dance. Never out of my sight."*

Sara nodded that she understood but when Bret offered to interpret, Steve agreed. Now as he spoke, Sara watched Bret's fluent ASL. *Never out of his sight, Sara. Two of the three leads aren't panning out.* Bret stopped long enough to shake his head. *I can't believe I've been one of those suspects all week.*

Steve circled his heart in apology, but continued as Bret signed for him. *M-I-K-E might show up at the dance or he might start something up again. Or it could be somebody else. Anything could happen. I think you both know that.*

It made Sara uneasy that their only plan was to keep her safely out of harm's way, but it was a start. To change her focus, she showed Bret the substitute dress she'd picked for the dance. It was dark green, flattering, especially since there were no razor cuts in it. Regretfully, she walked Bret to the apartment door.

*We've been through so much together already, Sara. I can't believe you'd think I'd ever do anything to hurt you.* He kissed her at the door. It was a kiss she wanted to remember forever.

Friday at Radley Academy was as uneventful as the rest of the week had been. Except for the fact that Rosemary Marino was acting like a permanent member of the faculty, the school day was the way it should always be. Either the stalker somehow knew of the police surveillance, or Mike Lenza was the stalker and simply not in the building all day. It didn't matter which might turn out to be the truth. It didn't matter if the stalker was an alien. Sara's nerves were permanently jangled. On edge, she thought bitterly, was the perfect way to describe it. She was constantly on the brink of anxiety, butterflies, jumping out of her skin. Sara put another picture of Tuck in the empty spot in her locker primarily because she missed him so, but also because it gave her a small feeling of control.

She ate lunch with her friends in the cafeteria, all of whom were going to the dance.

Liz and her committee would begin to decorate the minute the final bell rang. Sara sat and caught most of what was said about the plans, the deejay, and the outfits everyone was wearing.

As they got up to leave, Liz tapped her arm. "Look, Sara, there's something you need to know. My date tonight is Mike Lenza."

Sara's heart did its usual thump. "Mike?"

"I know you told me to stay away from him last week, but you can't have him and Bret, too. Frankly, I don't even know if Mike said he'd go with me just because you're going to be there. I know he asked you out for tonight. I know he —"

She looked desperately at Keesha. *Say again.*

Keesha translated it into ASL.

"Liz, you shouldn't."

"You're being selfish. It isn't fair to Mike, either. Frankly, he didn't even want me to tell you."

Sara looked at Keesha who grimaced and pushed her bent index and middle fingers forward: *selfish.*

Not selfish, stalked, Sara wanted to cry. She couldn't tell her friends. Instead she nodded that she understood and tried to appear apologetic. "It's fine if you go with Mike, just be careful."

Liz looked at Keesha, assuming she'd misunderstood. When she realized she hadn't, she glared. "What's that supposed to mean?"

*Nothing.* Sara dropped her hands. "Forget it."

Steve's news when she got home from school was that Tuck was well enough to come home in the morning and was expected to recover fully. There was no permanent damage, but the poison had been identified, as they had suspected, as over-the-counter rat poison. Her brother added that it would be filed at the station along with everything else. He'd already taken the cake to the crime lab for prints and analysis.

Keesha and Jason were going out to dinner and driving with Marcus and his date. Although they'd made plans to go together, Keesha accepted Sara's explanation of going with Steve and Marisa instead. *What does it matter? We'll all wind up at the same place anyway.*

Sara piled her hair in a sophisticated knot, and wore makeup that highlighted her eyes. She wished there were some magic blush that could eliminate worry lines. Terror lines, she thought as she looked in the mirror.

Steve had agreed to drive and first they picked up Marisa. Sara knew her brother was as tense as she was, but the minute he looked at Marisa, he smiled.

She's good for him, Sara thought, and a good sport to go to two high school functions, two weekends in a row. They walked to the car holding hands, and hardly looked older than college students. It wasn't the first time she wondered how serious they were about each other or if Steve ever had time to think about anything besides his police cases — or the trouble his sister kept getting into.

Did Marisa worry as much as she did about the situations Steve put himself in? Does she know about mine? Sara sighed and moved into the backseat. Compared to her life, Steve's was a bed of roses.

As a chaperon, Steve had said the committee members asked him to be forty-five minutes early, which suited him fine. Liz and Mike would most likely be there early, too. Steve hadn't been any more enthusiastic about Liz's date than Sara, but he agreed that it would give him a chance to observe the suspect in normal surroundings.

When they reached the Sandersons', Sara went up to the door. Bret opened it the minute she knocked. She stayed long enough to sign to his parents, then moved willingly into the crook of his arm as he wrapped it around her. Later, she thought, she'd tell him how wonderful it felt to know she could trust him.

At 6:45 P.M. they parked in the nearly empty school lot and entered through the gym lobby. As Kim and Liz had promised, the gym had been transformed with pumpkins, cornstalks, bushels of apples, and streamers in fall colors.

A school administrator was always required to be present and tonight it was Brenda Fletcher, along with her husband, John, in the corner helping the deejay set up his table. Marcus and Keesha weren't there yet. One of the advantages of having your guardian be twenty-two instead of a parent was that it wasn't nearly as embarrassing to walk into a school gym with him. Especially when he was bent on saving your life.

Kim and her date, senior Luke Fallon, and members of the committee were milling around setting up the refreshments and taking care of last-minute arrangements. For a few, brief moments things felt ordinary. It felt wonderful to stand on the polished floor and feel a little relaxed again. All of it shattered however when Liz and Mike arrived. Sara's hands began to sweat and she breathed in short, small gasps to keep her anxiety at bay.

## Chapter 25

Bret guided her to the couple and stuck his hand out to Mike before she could object. They introduced themselves, made inane conversation about their respective basketball teams. Sara smiled at Liz, who gave her a half-smile in return. Steve was watching, too.

Bret tapped her shoulder. *We're so early, show me where Kim's backpack and the bulletin board were.*

Sara told Steve exactly where she was going and promised to be back in less than five minutes. He nodded and turned back to Mike, who wasn't even looking in their direction.

As Sara lead Bret down the hall past her

own locker she pointed to Kim's. *She left her article over there while she went to the office.*

Bret sighed. *No wonder I got blamed. I came in through the gym and asked about you. The students who told me you'd gone were right here. They must have seen you at your locker with Mike.*

*More than at my locker. I walked him down the hall to the gym office on my way out to meet Kim. Meet Kim, Bret.*

*I know, I know. I just didn't know then. I stood here trying not to get angry. There was a paper clip in my pocket.* He swore and shook his head. *I stood right here and bent it back and forth while I tried to decide whether to call you later or just forget it. The undercover cop must have seen me here. Funny, I never saw her. I would have recognized her right away.*

*She didn't want to be seen,* Sara replied. While they were there she opened her locker and showed him the replaced photo of Tuck. *Want to come with us when we pick him up tomorrow? He's right down the street from your house.*

*It's a date,* he replied with his hands.

When she'd closed her locker, Sara led Bret to the administration corridor. Although the lights were on, it was off-limits and she stayed just long enough to point out the now-empty bulletin board. Every Friday it was stripped so new articles could go up Monday morning.

*There's nothing to show you, but that's where the article was last week until somebody saw that it had been stabbed full of holes and took it down so I wouldn't feel bad.* The painfully familiar lurch of her heart made her breath catch. She stepped closer. As if she didn't trust her eyesight, she ran her hand over the surface. *Bret, there aren't any holes in the board! If the article had been punctured the way Mrs. Fletcher described it, the holes would be here, pencil holes, traces of graphite . . . something!*

*Did she say someone took it off the board?*

*I don't remember, I just assumed since that's where it had been. . . .* Without another word, she grabbed Bret's hand and ran the length of the hallway to the gym. Dance committee students were arriving now, milling around, laughing. She found

Keesha's mother shaking hands with a sophomore.

*Help me, if she doesn't understand,* she signed to Bret. "Mrs. Fletcher, I have a question about the article with the holes in it."

Keesha's mother immediately turned apologetic. "I'm so sorry about that, Sara."

Sara waved away the apology. "Where was it?"

Brenda looked confused and Bret repeated the question.

"It was the one from the bulletin board outside the business office."

"I know." Sara's heart raced with impatience. "But when you saw it, was it up there still?"

"No. No, I had a finance meeting in the business office and I saw it on our work/study student's desk — her name's Deanna Margate. When she saw how shocked I was she explained that she'd seen it and taken it down."

*Thank you,* Sara signed.

Keesha's mother put her hand on her arm. "Don't let it ruin your night."

"No. No, I won't." Sara walked with Bret

to the corner of the room. *She didn't take it down damaged. There were no holes in the bulletin board. What if D-E-A-N-N-A M-A-R-G-A-T-E took the article off the bulletin board, punched the holes, and was about to put it back when Keesha's mom happened to see it? She'd have to cover herself, so she'd lie and say she'd taken it down damaged. She'd taken it down clean and was going to put it back up damaged, is more likely. Do you think she's the one? Do you think she's done all the other things?*

It made no sense. Then again, nothing she'd been through made sense. She tried to think. Deanna Margate. The name was as unfamiliar as her face. A college student in the business office . . . Then Sara remembered. Deanna was the woman who had given her the 3x5 notecards. She'd been nasty to her, and she'd known who Sara was. Sara looked at Bret as if he could give her answers.

Bret slowed her down with a wave of his hand. *How would she know about Tuck?*

*She knew about Tuck because he's been here with me. Not only that, but all the frightening things stopped at school when Steve put a tail on me, when R-O-S-E-M-A-R-Y was here. D-E-A-N-N-A would have known because she works in the business office. That's why she started stalking me at home.* Chills shot through Sara. The business office, of course! *Bret, she could have sabotaged my reservations for the regatta. I almost didn't go because they lost my file.*

Bret picked up her shorthand. *If she's the one, she could have easily left the rose that Sunday night. It would have been easy to follow you and slice the dress the minute you were out of the cleaners' . . . or sneak into your building. No one cares if you're college-age and look okay. The only thing that's missing is the* why. *Why Sara? Do you know her?*

*I just saw her that once in the business office. Tuck is easy. There are pictures of everything that's important to me in my locker. All she'd have to do is open it to get some idea of what to go after to scare me. Tuck came to school; she could put the poison out where I walked him every day.*

They turned together to try to find Steve. Steve, however, was nowhere to be found.

After a quick glance at the refreshment area, she went back to Brenda Fletcher and asked about her brother.

"He and Mike Lenza are doing last-minute errands in the parking lot. Sara, I'm sure you'd rather that he and Marisa go along to a movie or something, but they're welcome to stay if they'd like."

Sara frowned. "He's a chaperon tonight. Has to stay."

Brenda shook her head. "No, there must be a mistake. I made the arrangements. I called Kyle Miller's parents." She pointed to a couple who were still in the lobby. "They just arrived."

"There wasn't someone on the committee who called and asked him to be here forty-five minutes early?"

"Not that I know of." *No. Sorry.*

Sara tried to think. Steve had said he'd been told to be early. She signed as she hurried with Bret. *This woman — D M-A-R-G-A-T-E could have called to get him to chaperon. She set him up. Now he's with M-I-K-E, probably thinking he's keeping me safe by keeping us separated.*

She turned breathlessly to Marisa. "Marisa, has Steve ever mentioned the name Margate?"

Marisa frowned. "Martinson, your friend?"

"Margate," Bret repeated for her.

She looked troubled. "He doesn't talk about his work much. He can't most of the time, but Margate . . . Margate." Her eyes widened. "Last spring, Sara, one of the nights I saw your brother at the emergency room, he'd come in with a robbery suspect he'd arrested. Steve was dressed in horrible old clothes. He muttered that he'd been undercover for weeks on this case. You were at school. Tobias Margate had been shot in the process of holding up a bank in City Square."

"Could you be mistaken about the name?" Bret asked.

She shook her head. "I did the paperwork, the police report from his admissions file at the hospital. I remember the name — unusual. A few weeks ago Steve mentioned that he had to go to court for the sentencing. I'm sure it was Tobias Margate. That was the afternoon Steve had his tires slashed. In fact, I think he said he even met the guy's sister a few times at the Side Door Café last winter to try and get information from her. She's a college student."

Bret took her hands. "Marisa, do you know why you and Steve are here tonight? Why you came to my game last Friday?"

She grew serious. "I know only what he tells me: that someone's been harassing Sara. Of course I know about Tuck." Her expression changed. "You think Margate is connected to this?"

Sara nodded. "Deanna Margate works here at school. I think she poisoned Tuck. I think she arranged to have Steve chaperon. Watch for Mike and Steve. The minute they come in, get my brother, tell him what you know. Go stand with the Fletchers." Mike Lenza appeared at the door with a case of soda. "There they are now. Bret and I will call nine-one-one. The phone's right in the hall outside the gym. Can you understand me?"

Marisa nodded.

For the second time Sara led Bret down the narrow interior entrance past the locker rooms to the hall. She glanced at her locker. It was ajar and bits of paper lay on the floor in front of it. *Hold on a minute,* she signed, already scrambling for a closer look.

She pulled back the narrow metal door. The new photo of Tuck had been sliced. A clean, sharp *X* ran from corner to corner. The picture of Steve on the ski slope that Mike Lenza had stared at was shredded. Pieces lay on the floor, and on top of the books at the bottom of the  locker. None of it made her scream. The cry came when she saw the smear of blood that ran from the top of the inside of the locker door across the pictures.

# Chapter 26

The metal dug into her as she spun to Bret. *She's here! It's Steve! She never hurt me because she was terrifying me to unnerve Steve. Steve is the one she's after. She's been stalking, frightening me because Steve had arrested her brother. I know it.*

Bret grabbed her by the shoulders, then let go. *You know he would do anything she wants to try and protect you and the rest of us.*

Sara bit her lip. *I know. But the first thing he'd do is try to get her out of the building. Maybe he could reason with her if they knew each other. God, Bret, how do you reason with somebody who's sliced your tires, poisoned your dog, and stalked your sister?*

*You get her to talk. Tell me how you did it,*

*D-E-A-N-N-A. How did you ever poison Tuck? That kind of thing.*

Sara looked up at the red glow of the EXIT sign at the end of the corridor. *He'd get her to show him how or where she did it. He'd play hero and get her out of here. She'd take him out to the soccer field. I'm sure that's where she laid the poison. That's where I walked Tuck at lunch.*

Bret did his best to reassure her. *This is his job, Sara. He'll get her just away from the parking lot, far enough to subdue her without hurting anybody else. He's a big guy. He can handle a college student.*

*He's unarmed. If this is his blood, he's bleeding.* She pounded the locker where the blood streaked across the picture. *Call 911. Tell them no sirens. They can't scare her. She's got to be crazy. I'll meet you out there.*

*Wait for me! You're not going anywhere without me.*

*No time. I'm not in danger, Steve is. Hurry!* Before Bret could argue, she raised her hands, signed *911,* and ran to the fire door. The November air made her gasp, but she kept going, running her hand along the bricks. It couldn't be more than seven-thirty. On the other side of the wall, the deejay was probably starting his first song. Her friends might be looking for her, but it would take at least a half hour for everyone to arrive and the dance to get into full swing.

Even on moonless, overcast nights like this one, night in Radley was rarely pitch-black. Streetlights rimmed the campus and bright city lights filled the sky with a hazy glow. She headed for the soccer field. It was the perfect spot for Deanna: dark; long grassy stretches on either side; hundreds of yards to the nearest street in all directions.

Well off to her right, on the other side of the gym, headlights shone as cars began to fill the student lot. A single scream would bring them all running. She had on low-heeled dress shoes that sank in the damp grass. Nevertheless, she began to run. A single scream might send Deanna Margate completely over the edge, as well.

There was no sign of Deanna or Steve. She walked every place she'd been with Tuck. Her pulse pounded painfully. There wasn't time to debate any of it. She needed to get back to Bret and wait for the police, but she'd be useless if she couldn't discover where Steve had taken Deanna. Or where Deanna had taken Steve. Desperately she looked everywhere again. She'd been wrong. Dangerously wrong.

Ten years of deafness had sharpened all her other senses. Her nostrils flared. Cigarettes. Was Deanna smoking? Steve didn't. Sara stood still and scanned the field. The odor was faint, barely noticeable, but as she turned, she saw a tiny gold glow in the furthest corner of the campus. She walked carefully. The tiny glow disappeared, only to appear again as she approached. She squinted. Dark forms were barely noticeable up against the soccer goal cage that had been moved into the corner, off the field, for the last mowing of the year.

As she walked, the light flicked into the air, sailing in a graceful arc and landing in the dirt. Deanna had her back to her. She sat upright, cross-legged on the grass in a hooded black sweatshirt and dark pants. No wonder she hadn't been visible. Steve was leaning against the goal in his shirt and tie.

It was too dark to read Steve's lips. It was impossible to tell if he was making progress with Deanna, or just biding his time while he thought of a plan. Look up, she prayed. The police would be here any minute. I'll direct them, Steve. Keep her calm for ten more minutes. There had only been a trace of blood, superficial. As soon as the squad car arrived, Steve could just get up and walk Deanna to the waiting officers. They could take her to the psychiatric ward for the attention she needed.

How many times had Steve warned her not to involve herself in police work? He was driven by knowledge and practice: a college degree in criminal justice, training at the academy, months in the field. She was driven by her adrenaline, which suddenly surged again.

Deanna moved. Sara dropped to her knees and crawled closer. The woman leaned forward and pulled her lighter from her pocket. The flame hissed and flickered. Sara jammed her fist to her mouth. Her brother's shirt was dark with blood. He shot his arm into the air and grabbed for Deanna's wrist, not for the lighter. Deanna kept that poised. He'd reached for her other hand, the one that held a blade over his chest. The effort made him slump forward then back as he slid heavily against the post and lay still.

There was no time left for strategy or patience. Sara threw herself across Deanna's back, knocking her forward into the dirt. The knife sailed into the dark. Deanna tensed and pushed Sara off as she managed to struggle to her feet. She moved again for Steve, then froze. Then suddenly, Marisa was running to him. As Sara regained her balance, Deanna darted across the playing field toward the street.

Blue lights swam in the distance, followed by the violent blinking of red. They ignored Bret, Sara thought vaguely as she raced. Maybe they knew they were coming for one of their own. Maybe they thought the force had lost enough Howells. Her lungs screamed but the effort was no worse than her crewing workout. Unless Deanna Margate rowed for Radley University, Sara was in far better shape. She kicked off her shoes and sprinted in the dark, then lunged with a final burst and caught Deanna across the back, sending her flying again into the grassy stretch of the soccer field. She held her down despite the struggle until arms stronger than hers pulled her off. Uniformed officers had appeared out of the dark, none that she recognized, or maybe she knew them all.

Someone shook her firmly. His mouth moved but she couldn't understand. She resisted until she saw that Deanna had been handcuffed. They were both led to the police car in the lighted parking lot.

"Why?" Sara asked Deanna as tears choked her already muffled voice. "Why?"

Deanna's features were distorted by hate and the glare of the headlight from the squad car. "Did you think I'd just sit back and let your brother ruin my life? The great detective ... trying to get information out of me ... pretending to like me ... always pretending. Your brother never liked me. He took Toby; he took everything. Toby was paying for college. Toby was going to make us rich." She shook her hair from her eyes.

"What am I without my brother? I had to get a part-time job and what does it turn out to be? This stupid school. . . . Don't you see? I came here last month and who's a student? You! It was like a sign. The Howells, right under my nose, the perfect brother and sister. Not anymore. Better than slicing tires. I started with that stupid regatta. I wish you'd drowned."

Sara lunged. An officer pulled her back. Deanna went on, unable to stop, tears rolling down her face. "I did it all. I made the calls and left the rose and the leash and the cake. And, yes, I poisoned Tuck. I wanted you to pay as I had paid."

An officer put Deanna in the back of the squad car.

*"I know she's crazy, but she poisoned Tuck. She's been out here trying to murder Steve. She can't." She can't,* Sara added with elbows flying as she shook off the officer who still restrained her. *"She can't have my dog and she can't have my brother."* She tapped her chest as she panted. They're mine, she wanted to add. They're all I have. She turned to look back across the field.

\*   \*   \*

For what seemed like hours, Sara had been staring at the folded, blood-soaked Radley Academy gym towels in the sink of the East End General Hospital's emergency room. Once he'd seen the blood on the locker, it was Bret who'd thought to get Marisa, who was a nurse, after he'd called the police. It was Marisa who'd grabbed the towels from the locker room before the two of them had raced out into the dark.

"No one in the gym even knew we were gone," Marisa was saying, "except Mike Lenza who stayed outside and directed the police once they arrived."

Sara circled her heart. *I owe him an apology,* she said and signed. *"Liz, too."*

*"Almost as big as the one you owed me,"* Bret replied.

They were all behind the curtain that separated Steve's bed from the others that filled the room. The police had finally left and the physicians were finished. He lay under a single sheet, sutured and bandaged from shoulder to ribs, saved by the fact that Deanna Margate hadn't managed to hit anything more vital than muscle and Marisa had the training and forethought to use the towels as compresses to slow the bleeding until they reached the hospital. Steve was groggy from the medication, but determined to go home.

"Some date you are," Marisa said as she held his hand. "My big night off and I wind up right back where I spent the day."

His grin was lopsided. "I wanted to make sure I got first-class service. Everything depends on who you know in a place like this." He winced but as he closed his eyes he made a waving motion with his hands.

Marisa walked Bret and Sara into the hall. Her smile was kind. "Sara, even in the ambulance all Steve worried about was keeping you out of this emergency room. I know it has terrible memories for you."

Sara stopped her before she could go on about the death of her father. "I'm all right, really."

Marisa smiled. "If it helps, think of it as the place where Steve and I met. He's an incredible person, Sara. You're lucky to have him watching over you."

"That's all I could think about when I was

keeping Deanna away from him." She shook her head at the condition of her dress, so torn they'd given her a lab coat to put on over it. Her knuckles were bandaged and a bruise had formed on her temple. "I know she needs help. She blamed Steve for everything."

"I know," Marisa replied. "Steve said getting even was all she talked about from the minute he ran into her in the hall by your locker until he passed out at the soccer cage."

*"She even followed me to the regatta. High Pines. I felt it! All weekend. Blamed it on Mike."*

"Well tonight while Mike brought in the soda, Steve took a quick search of the locker rooms. When he came out, he caught Deanna slicing up the pictures at your locker. He recognized her. He convinced her to go outside and talk. That's when she attacked him."

"But he'll recover?" Sara asked.

Marisa knit her eyebrows.

*"He'll be okay?"*

*Yes,* she signed back. "It may be a few more hours, and of course I'll have to make some house calls, but I'll bring him home as soon as they let me. He'll be fine. You'll have

Tuck and Steve as overprotective as ever. You guys go on."

When they finally left, Sara looked up at Bret who was as exhausted as she was, if cleaner. *Even though I fought the idea till the end, I can't believe I ever thought you were part of this.*

*My timing was horribly perfect. I don't blame you. I almost forget what it's like to date a girl who leads a regular life. Very boring, I guess.*

Sara smiled in the harsh light of the waiting area. *This is the second time I've blown my chance to dance.*

They'd reached the exit, but instead of heading back toward her car, Bret tugged her over to a scrap of landscaping between the parking lot and the emergency room entrance. He straightened the lapels of her white lab coat and pulled her into his arms.

"What are you doing?"

He looked at her so she could read his lips. "Dancing."

"There's no deejay!" As she spoke she felt the tap, tap, tap, tap; one, two, three, four as

Bret drummed the rhythm on her shoulder. She moved into his arms and looked up into his handsome face.

He grinned at her. "Since when do we need anything but our own music?"

———————⬤———————

*When asked to help out at a lavish fund-raiser at the Radley Museum, Sara is part of a glittering world of priceless jewels, glamorous people . . . and* death.

*Read* Hear No Evil #4: DEAD AND BURIED

# What could Sara have that a thief wants?

## Every day Sara Howell faces mystery, danger ... and silence.

After Sara discovers the body of a museum security guard, her world turns upside-down: First her vacation condo is ransacked. Then her apartment back in Radley is robbed. What could the thieves be after, and how long before they come after Sara herself?

# HEAR NO EVIL #4

## Dead and Buried

### Kate Chester

Coming soon to a bookstore near you.

# MED CENTER

**A building blows up . . .
and Med Center's volunteers
feel the shock waves.**

It's bad enough that Med Center is crowded
with victims of a chemical explosion. But
worse yet, many of the wounded are still
trapped inside the building. Is it worth it for
the Med Center volunteers to risk their lives
in a dangerous rescue attempt?

BLAST

## MED CENTER #4

### BY DIANE HOH

**Their lives are nonstop drama . . .
inside the hospital and out.**

**Coming soon to a bookstore near you.**

MC396